blue

The Tig

LEIGH DOUGLASS BRACKETT was born in Los Angeles. Her first love was science fiction and she was a great fan in her youth of Edgar Rice Burroughs' Tarzan and John Carter Martian stories. Her first story, 'Martian Quest', was published in *Astounding Science Fiction* in 1940, but her first novel was *No Good From A Corpse* (1944), a tough-minded and realistic thriller in the Raymond Chandler tradition which few at the time realised was written by a woman.

On the strength of the novel, she was brought to Hollywood where she worked with William Faulkner and Jules Furthman on the script of Howard Hawks' film version of Chandler's *The Big Sleep*. She became one of Hawks' favoured screenwriters, responsible in later years for the screenplays of *Rio Bravo* (1959), *Hatari!* (1961), *El Dorado* (1967) and *Rio Lobo* (1970), curiously all films about male bonding. Other notable screen credits include another Chandler adaptation, Robert Altman's *The Long Goodbye* (1973), and the second *Star Wars* movie, *The Empire Strikes Back* (1979).

Her only other crime books are *The Tiger Among Us* (1957), a harrowing precursor of the vigilante yarn, *Silent Partner* (1969) and *Stranger at Home* (1946) which she ghost-wrote for actor George Sanders.

She is better remembered for countless short stories and fourteen volumes of science fiction which include classics like *The Sword of Rhiannon* (1953), *The Big Jump* (1955) and *The Long Tomorrow* (1955). Equally at ease in diverse popular genres, Leigh Brackett was also awarded the Spur Award for the best Western for *Follow the Free Wind* (1963).

Happily married to science fiction writer Edmond Hamilton from 1946 to his death in 1977, she survived him barely a year and died in 1978.

Series Editor: Maxim Jakubowski

blue murder

blue murder

THE TIGER AMONG US

Leigh Brackett

SIMON & SCHUSTER

LONDON • SYDNEY • NEW YORK • TOKYO • TORONTO

First published in 1957
First published as a Blue Murder paperback by
Simon & Schuster Limited 1989

Simon & Schuster Ltd
West Garden Place
Kendal Street
London W2 2AQ

Simon & Schuster of Australia Pty Ltd
Sydney

British Library Cataloguing-in-Publication Data available

ISBN 0–671–65283–4

Printed and bound in Great Britain by
Richard Clay Ltd, Bungay, Suffolk

THE TIGER AMONG US

1

In several places I have used the word "tiger" in connection with Chuck and his pals. It might seem that that was merely an attempt to be dramatic, and maybe it was when I wrote it, but it is also, I think, a symbolic truth.

These were "boys" only by an arbitrary definition, and they were "juvenile delinquents" only by accident. Their urges had nothing to do with overcrowded slums, or broken homes, or submerged minorities. Those are social problems, but the thing that drove these boys is older than society, as old and as deep as the roots of the human race. Theirs was the problem of the tiger that is always among us, the immemorial tiger whose first given name was Cain.

That tiger is always young. His crimes are the crimes of youth, and they seem to be multiplying these days. Perhaps this is partly because of our laissez-faire attitude toward the young. Or perhaps it is only because the population is bigger and so there are numerically more of these violent children who grow up to be violent men. Young men, eighteen, twenty, twenty-five years old. By that time they are nearly always caught. There are few old men in the ranks of the thrill seekers, the sadists, and the compulsive slayers.

But before they're caught, a lot of innocent people have suffered. Pick up any newspaper, any day, anywhere, and you're likely to find at least one account of the sort of crime I'm talking about. Unless it's an unusually spectacular one, it is customarily dealt with in half a dozen lines or so. The article gives the name of the victim and his address and whether he lived or died, and that's all, and unless you happen to know him personally you shake your head briefly over the wickedness of the world and turn to the baseball scores.

For the victim and the victim's family, it's not that easy. The tiger has mauled and marked them for all time.

I can give you a firsthand account of that because I was a six-line item on Page One.

I was a victim.

My name is Walter Sherris. I live in Mall's Ford, Ohio, a steel town close to the Pennsylvania line.

Eighteen months ago I was thirty-one years old. I was healthy. I had a solid job with a future. I had a nice home in the suburbs with no more mortgage than most people have, and a practically new hard-top almost half paid for. I have the prettiest brightest wife in the county, a three-year-old daughter that was the image of her, and a little boy just past his first birthday. I was all set.

Then one spring night I took a walk.

My job was in the credit department of Valley Steel Fabricators, Inc. I worked late that night getting the accounts in shape for the semi-annual audit. It was warm and lonesome, and about ten-thirty I decided I needed a break.

Old Schmitz let me out the front door. I told him I was going for coffee and to look for me back in about fifteen minutes. My car was on the lot beside the building, but I left it there. The twenty-four-hour truck stop on the corner of Route 18 was only two blocks away, and I wanted the walk more than I did the coffee.

Valley Steel is on a curving by-pass called Williams Avenue, some little way out from the centre of town. I began to walk north. The air smelled moist and green with the fresh rankness of weeds growing in the open spaces. From up ahead I could hear the rumble of the big semis going through on the highway. There was no traffic on Williams. It serves the plants that are on it, and few people use it except during the morning and evening rush. There was a cluster of lights far behind me marking an overpass, and there were lights two blocks ahead at

8

the corner, but in between there was only night, with no moon showing.

In a minute or two I heard a car coming up Williams from the direction of town.

I could hear it coming a long way off, because it was making that rushing, snarling, singing noise that means something special in the way of speed. Kids, I thought, and hoped they would be able to make their stop at the corner. The beam of their headlights picked me up, and I saw my shadow racing round clockwise over the pavement, over the weeds, into darkness again. Then all of a sudden the brakes went on. Tires slewed on the asphalt with a long screeching moan. The car went lurching and skidding past me, and I realized that the driver had cut his lights. Then it pulled in sharp ahead of me and stopped, with one front wheel cocked up on the curb.

It was a convertible, some lightish color that might have been gray, blue, or green, with a dark top, a souped-up job with two shiny tail pipes. The motor was still running. I could hear laughter from inside, the kind of wild brainless laughter kids will get off sometimes when they're worked up to a pitch of excitement. There was a fast gabble of talk, and then some pushing and jostling, and five boys piled out of the convertible and stood around me.

Just boys. Kids. Youngsters. It sounds so helpless and appealing that way. But only one of them was shorter than I, a broad chunky type. Two of them were fully my size. Another was tall and skinny, and the fifth topped me by four inches and must have outweighed me by at least twenty pounds. I couldn't see any of their faces. They were only five dim shapes hemming me in. And now I was beginning to be just a little bit scared.

"Well," I said, "what do you want?"

The big one stood directly in front of me, so that I had to stop or run into him.

"I want to know where you're going," he said, and the others all laughed as though he had said something quite clever. "Where are you going, tramp?"

"Look," I said. "You boys have no quarrel with me."

"That's for us to say, tramp," said the big one. He put his

9

hand quickly on my chest and shoved. I gave back a step and one of the others pushed me from behind, and then they all had a shove, scuffling their feet on the pavement, laughing. I kept my hands at my sides.

"I asked you," said the big one. "Where you going, tramp?"

"I don't know when that got to be any of your business," I said, "but I'm going for a cup of coffee. Does that satisfy you?"

"A cup of coffee," said one of the others, mimicking. They all laughed. Then the tall skinny one said a little doubtfully, "I thought you said he had to be a tramp, Chuck. He don't sound like one to me."

"What else would he be?" said the big one. "Unless he's a crook. Are you a crook, crook?"

The stocky boy laughed a loud silly laugh.

"Listen," I said, keeping my hands down, keeping my voice quiet and reasonable. "I'm not a tramp and I'm not a crook. I'm just a guy trying to make a living. I'm not doing you any harm. Now why don't you go on and find something better to do?"

"Shut up," said Chuck. Suddenly he seemed to have gone into a rage. "I'm sick of people telling me what to do. All night they've been telling me, go here, go there, get out. The hell with you. Shut up!"

The others shuffled their feet but they did not laugh now, except for the stocky boy, and even he had changed his tone.

Chuck said to me softly, stepping close, "I'm bigger than you are."

"Physically, yes. So what?"

"So I don't have to do anything you tell me."

Now I laughed. This was perhaps not a smart thing to do, but it looked like the only chance I had. "If you're such a giant, why do you have to have four other guys to back you up against one?" I turned to the others. "What do you want to let him get you into trouble for? Use your heads. This isn't——"

"Shut up," said Chuck, with a peculiarly nasty quietness. "I told you."

He hit me. He was as strong as a horse. I stumbled back into the others, and they began to bounce me around. Have you any idea what it feels like to be in that particular spot? You're a grown man and these are boys. You feel degraded to be afraid of them but you are afraid. You feel outraged because they have laid hands on you for no reason except that they just felt like it. You feel that they're protected by all sorts of laws and customs and that it is somehow not right to fight them, even in self-defense, as you would fight grown men. And yet there they are, grown men in everything but mind, able to wound, able to destroy.

You want to kill them. This is a feeling you do not ask for or plan on having. It just comes.

Several people have said that what happened then was my fault.

I began to hit back. I yelled as loud as I could, hoping Schmitz or somebody might hear me. He didn't hear me. No one did. Shut him up, Chuck said, and they shut me up. In a few seconds I was down on the ground with all five of them on top of me, and my mouth was full of blood.

Keep him there, said Chuck's voice. Who does he think *he* is?

He isn't any tramp.

Who cares?

Hey. Hey, Chuck, could he be a cop?

Cop? No, why should he be a cop? I told you, he's nobody. Let's look at his wallet, anyway.

All right, all right, chicken. Give it to me.

I rolled over on my face and got my knees under me.

Stay down, you. Didn't you hear what we said?

The world turned over again. Laughter. Hey, look, I should of worn my football shoes, these rubber soles just bounce. More laughter.

Chuck's voice talking. Hold the match so I can see. Walter Sherris, 202 Laurel Terrace—I told you hold the match, Bill, what's the matter?

Another voice. I got to go, Chuck. I got to go.

What's the matter, gutless, you know him or something?

Let me go, Chuck. I got to go!

It became important to see who Bill was. Tremendously

important. I wasn't sure why. I squirmed around. The night was very dark. Shapes moved in it. Fear moved in it. Pain moved in it. I saw a tall skinny shadow run to the convertible and jump in.

Now there were only four.

I took a deep breath.

Has he got any money?

The hell with his money. Who needs it?

The wallet slapped me sharply across the face.

There you are, *Mr.* Sherris. Laurel Terrace Drive. Well, well. No cop. No tramp, no crook. Just a real nice clean white-collar type. Yes, sir, no, sir, and cut the lawn every Sunday. Look at him, fellas, that's what your mammas want you to grow up to be. Hey, goof, let's see that cigarette lighter.

A tiny star burned, high over my head.

Chuck had taken a picture out of my wallet. I knew what it was. That was easy, because I only carried one. It was a picture of Tracey and the children, taken last summer on our lawn.

They liked the picture of Tracey. They whistled.

Some dish.

You can have her. She's a type. Bet you do everything she tells you, don't you, *Mr.* Sherris? Every little damn thing. Dump the garbage, walk the dog, mow the lawn——

Chuck's voice had got high and sharp, mocking somebody I didn't know.

I tackled him.

It was like tackling a stone wall. He wasn't fat, or soft, or slow. He was just plain big, and muscled like a football player. Even so I think I hurt him, because he yelped and called me a dirty name in a tone of outraged surprise. Then all four of them were on me, beating me down, laughing, grunting, cursing.

Well, he means it, doesn't he?

Look out, damn you, that hurt.

Hey, goof, watch out who you're kicking, that was me.

We were off the pavement now, rolling and stomping in the cool wet weeds. There was a wheel close to my face. It had a white sidewall tire on it and a shiny hubcap. There was an emblem on the hubcap, but I couldn't see what it was. Please quit, I said. Please let me alone. My voice sounded very small. I don't think they heard it.

The hubcap and the white side-wall turned into a bumper and grille, seen foreshortened and stubby from underneath. Somebody was jumping, with both hands on the front of the car to help him. He was breathing hard. I could hear him breathing. He was jumping on me.

You know who this is? This is that crummy bartender.

Give him one for me.

No, I'll tell you who it is, it's that so-and-so outside on the corner, the one with the pink shirt.

Think they can push us around, do they?

Chuck didn't say who I was. But he knew. I was somebody he hated worse than the bartender, worse than the so-and-so with the pink shirt.

Voices, far, far away. After a while I knew they were not talking any more. They were making noises, like the noises dogs make when they have something cornered.

I lost track. I don't know when they decided to quit and go home.

2

TRACEY was telling me to cut the lawn. It's the worst-looking one in the neighborhood, dear, and the dandelions are really a disgrace. You must do something about it.

I ran the mower back and forth over the long grass. A green shower fell around it and the lawn lay short and smooth in a neat stripe under the spinning blades. Tracey watched me, smiling. She was wearing that orange sunsuit that made her look so cute and sexy I couldn't keep my mind on the grass, and her hair was bright gold, all curly around her head. Pudge was in his playpen. He was bouncing something up and down like a ball.

Tracey held up a silver lobster pick as big as a hand hoe. I've been working all afternoon in the flower beds, she said. Her nails were long, very long, very brilliantly red. Weeding is hard work, she said, and I said, it would be easier if you'd cut your nails short. She pouted at me with her pretty red mouth. Honey, she said, you don't want me to turn into a perfect frump, do you?

Pudge laughed a loud silly laugh. He was racing around the playpen bouncing this thing. It was not a ball at all. It was a man's head. The head had a big nose and long hair that floated up and down every time it bounced. He found it somewhere, said Tracey. Isn't he cute?

I ran the mower back and forth. It had white side-wall tires and a shiny grille, with headlights on the front. And that's ridiculous, I said, because who cuts the lawn on a Sunday *night*?

I'm going in, Tracey said. It's getting cold. Where's Bets? Bets! Come to mommy, dear, it's time to go inside.

Bets came running across the lawn. The lawn was a mile wide and it was getting dark and her little legs ran and ran. She was crying. There was blood running down her face, all down her front and splashing on her bare feet. Bad boys, she cried. The bad boys did it. I started toward her but it was very dark now and I couldn't see her any more. Pudge laughed his loud silly laugh. Where do you think you're going, tramp? he said, and I said, That's no way to talk to your father. Shut up, said Pudge. He was standing in front of me now. Shut up. He was huge in the night. He shoved me, and it wasn't Pudge at all, it was——

I yelled. A woman's voice spoke to me. I thought perhaps it was Tracey. The voice said everything was all right, and sure enough when I looked again everybody was gone and Tracey had taken the children into the house. It was dark and quiet. I felt sleepy. I slept.

There were other dreams. There were other moments of rising almost to the surface of the black pool I was sunk in, close enough for a dim glance at a room I didn't think was mine, for a dim feeling that things were somehow not good with me. Then one time I came all the way to the top and stayed there.

I was in the Southside unit of City Hospital. I had a fine view of the steel mills out the window. My left leg was in traction, I hurt all over, and somewhere at the back of my consciousness was that cold shivery feeling as of having walked too close to a precipice in the dark. I wanted Tracey. I wanted her awfully bad.

I did not get Tracey. I got my sister Mae, so genuinely glad to see me and so obviously relieved that I got even more scared.

"How long was I out?" I asked her.

"Oh, a couple of days." She hurried over that. "How do you feel?"

"Terrible." I ran my tongue around the inside of my mouth. The cuts were all healed and my lips weren't swollen. That was funny, but I was too tired to worry about it. "Where's Tracey?"

"Now, you don't have a doggone single thing to worry about, Walt." Mae leaned over and kissed me, brushing her soft brown hair over my cheek. "Tracey is fine, and so are the children."

"Sure," I said. "Why wouldn't they be fine? But where is Tracey? I want her."

"Walt," said Mae, looking down at me with her eyes full of suppressed fury, "who did this to you?"

"A bunch of kids."

Now her eyes came wide open in astonishment. "Kids!"

"Mae, where's Tracey? Why isn't she here?"

"What do you mean, Walt, a bunch of kids? Young fellows from around the plant, somebody with a grudge against you?"

"Just kids. I don't know who they were."

"You mean," she said slowly, "they were strangers, and they stopped and beat you up. Just like that."

"Mae——"

"But what *reason* did they have?"

"I don't know. It wasn't personal. Listen, give me a straight answer, will you? Where is Tracey?"

I watched a curtain come down over her face, leaving it closed and doubtful. She was thinking about something. This lasted only a second, and I wouldn't have caught it at all if it hadn't been that Mae's thought processes are perfectly transparent, and I've known every one of them since she was born.

"I guess you're right," she said. "You'll only fret more if I don't tell you. Tracey got a threatening letter, that's all. These boys must have known *something* about you."

Two-oh-two Laurel Terrace Drive, and cut the lawn every Sunday. Yes. And the tall skinny shadow that ran and hid in the car when it heard my name. Yes. My head was fuzzy and dim. It was hard to think.

"She got a letter?"

"Oh, it probably didn't mean anything, but Tracey thought it would be the wisest idea to take the children away for a while. It was for them, Walt. If it was just for herself wild horses wouldn't have dragged her, but you know how it is when you've got youngsters to think of."

"Where'd she go?"

"To Boston. To her uncle and aunt. She simply had to, Walt. For the children. She waited until she was sure——"

"Sure of what? Don't keep me hanging in mid-air, I feel lousy."

"Sorry, hon. Until she was sure you were out of danger. She telephones me every day. She'll be so happy——"

"Sure," I said. "Give her my love."

There was one of those awkward moments. Mae fidgeted, scrabbling in her handbag but not taking anything out, patting her hair. Beyond the window the buildings were dark with soot under a bright spring sky. The mill sheds were long and rusty black, and suddenly down the line one of the town's few remaining Bessemers began to spurt up a shaking pillar of flame.

"What did the letter say?"

"The usual things. It wasn't signed, of course. Tracey wasn't frightened for herself, it was just that she couldn't take a chance with Bets and Pudgy. I know exactly how she felt, with three of my own."

"Sure," I said. "Tell her she was right to go. Tell her I'm fine."

"Of course. She's been so terribly worried. Well, I guess I'd better go now. Doctor said five minutes was the limit. But I'll be back."

She kissed me again. There were tears welling up in her brown eyes. I loved her. But I wanted Tracey.

"When'll she be back?"

"Oh, soon. In a few days, when this is cleared up. The police will take care of it." She bent quickly and tried to hug me without touching anything. "I'm so happy I'm going to bawl. So long. See you tomorrow."

She left, digging for a handkerchief. I thought I must really have been in a bad way.

And Tracey was in Boston.

Two-oh-two Laurel Terrace Drive. I could hear Chuck's voice reading the address.

Of course she had had to go. It was for the children. The bad boys—no, that was part of the dream. But it was true. They mustn't touch Bets and Pudge. They mustn't touch Tracey either.

17

Of course she had had to go.

The Bessemer flared, throwing off beautiful flakes of fire.

I got nurses, rustling in and out, and I got the doctor. His name was Obermeyer, and he was Tracey's family doctor, one of the best in Mall's Ford and correspondingly expensive. He wouldn't tell me much except that I was fine and I mustn't worry.

I asked him about my leg.

"Fracture. Don't let all that traction stuff frighten you, it's mostly for show. Now I think we'll sleep again for a while."

We slept.

Next day I got Detective Koleski. He was a young fellow, neatly dressed in a dark blue suit. He was polite, businesslike, and thorough. We filled in some blanks for each other. Old Schmitz had got worried when I didn't come back. He called the truck stop, and when they told him I hadn't been there he came looking for me. By the time he found me I was all alone. He hadn't even seen the car.

"Could you identify the boys?" Koleski asked me.

I explained that I couldn't see their faces. "But I'd know the big one anywhere. I'd know his voice. His name was Chuck."

Koleski wrote it all down.

"Could you say how they were dressed?"

"Slacks. Jackets. It was dark, but I'd say they were well-dressed."

"Did they have any characteristics that might identify them as belonging to any particular population group?"

"No. They were all red-blooded American boys. And they weren't slum kids, either."

He glanced at me sharply. "What makes you so sure of that?"

"Driving a convertible?"

"They could have borrowed it."

"Or stolen it," I said, considering this new thought.

He shook his head. "No convertibles in the stolen-car complaints."

"Well, anyway, they weren't. They didn't talk like it nor act like it. They weren't interested in my money, and I had about forty bucks on me. The big one, Chuck, he was pretty bitter about suburbanites, but it was more a personal thing and not like class jealousy."

Every time I tried to think or remember, it started my head aching again, but I plugged on with it.

"He told the others to look at me, that was what their mammas wanted them to be. And the tall skinny one, Bill—he knew me, or knew who I was."

Koleski looked alert at that. He asked questions, writing fast. I couldn't think of any boy, offhand, that would fit Bill's description.

"I think they'd had trouble," I said. "With a bartender, and somebody in a pink shirt. Sounded as though they'd butted up against some real genuine toughies and had to turn tail and were taking out their spite on the first handy victim. They thought I was just a prowling tramp when they stopped."

"We'll check it out."

He got up to leave, and I said, "Wait a minute, what about that letter? Can't you tell anything from that?"

He gave me a blank look. "What letter?"

"The one they wrote to my wife."

"Oh," he said. "That letter. Well, to tell you the truth, Mr. Sherris, we haven't seen it."

"What do you mean, you haven't seen it? My wife——"

"She mentioned it. I questioned her, of course, regarding possible enemies you might have had, and she mentioned it. She said the letter had instructed her to burn it and she had burned it. So that doesn't give us very much to go on there."

"No," I said. "She was afraid for the children."

"I understand."

"Do you have any children?"

"No. I'm not married."

"Then you don't understand."

He nodded. "I guess I don't."

He could have meant a couple of things. I didn't ask him.

At the door he paused and said, "Try and think who the skinny boy might be. It would help a lot."

I said I would. He said he would keep me posted. He left.

I lay there trying to think about Bill, but I couldn't keep my mind on it. All I could think of was Tracey.

She didn't come, but her parents did. They were conventional people, a little stuffy for my taste, but nice. I liked them. But I wished they hadn't come. They looked as guilty and ill at ease as though they had been caught stealing my money, and it disturbed me. I couldn't see any reason for it. They certainly had not done me any harm.

3

K OLESKI came back again three days later.

"It doesn't come to much in the long run, Mr. Sherris, but I think I found out where your boys were when they had that beef you mentioned. Do you know the corner of Beekman and Front?"

"I've been through there." It lies just by the end of the East bridge, and it's the toughest corner in Mall's Ford, the heart of our slum district. Our slums are not very large, because Mall's Ford is not a very big city, but in their small compass they're as good as you can find anywhere.

"Well, there's a bar and grill called Noddy's. It's not exactly an elegant place, but Noddy's no fool. He makes good money and he wants to hang onto his license. We never have any trouble with him. So that night five boys came in shortly after ten o'clock. Noddy described them as smart alecks from uptown, a type he has met before and does not love. They go slumming, you know what I mean? And nobody likes to be slummed."

Koleski consulted his notebook. He was a methodical young man, more like a schoolteacher than a cop.

"There doesn't seem to be any doubt that it was the same five boys. The descriptions fit—the tall skinny boy, the short one with the loud laugh, the big one who seemed to be the leader. They were celebrating the big one's birthday."

He looked at me.

"His eighteenth birthday, Mr. Sherris. That puts him out of the juvenile class."

"About time," I said. "He's bigger and brighter than a lot of men I know. What about the others?"

"Noddy figured them in the sixteen-seventeen-year-old group. Old enough to know better. Well, anyway, they swaggered in and demanded drinks. Noddy told them he doesn't serve minors. The big one laughed and said a joint like Noddy's would serve anybody. Noddy told them to leave. The big one became very insolent and abusive, the others backing him up. Noddy threatened to call the cops, and the boys finally did go out. That's when the real trouble nearly started."

I waited. I was feeling a little better, a little more alive. I could hate with some real coherence.

"You know that part of town," said Koleski. "It's a regular League of Nations, and Noddy caters to them all. On a warm night there's always a pretty well-mixed bunch hanging around the corner. The big boy made a crack, and somebody—probably your guy in the pink shirt—decided not to let it pass. In two seconds there was the beginning of a race riot, and the boys got scared. They ran."

"Fine," I said. "So they worked it off on me. Did you get their names?"

He shook his head. "Fuller descriptions, that's all. And I'm afraid that isn't much. There are thousands of boys in Mall's Ford and the suburbs. Eliminate half of them and the descriptions would still fit the other half. The worst of it is, Mr. Sherris, that you yourself can't give us a positive identification."

"I'll bet I could."

Koleski looked doubtful. I knew he was thinking of courtrooms and attorneys.

"All right," I said. "But this Noddy—he saw their faces."

"He's not the complaining witness. And he didn't see them beating you."

"So," I said, "they're just going to get away with it."

"I didn't say that. I was only pointing out the difficulties."

"Difficulties," I said. I tried to sit up. It hurt like the devil, and that made me madder than ever. "Difficulties! Listen, I found out something this morning. I found out I was unconscious for nine days. They didn't know if I'd ever come out of it. They didn't know if I'd be normal, mentally or physically, if I did come out of it. They——"

"I know, Mr. Sherris," said Koleski. He was trying to soothe me down. "We'll do everything possible——"

I drowned him out. I was thinking of the darkness and the wet green weeds, the fear and the pain, the utter injustice. He could be calm about it. He could be sensible. He hadn't been there.

"They nearly killed me," I said. "For no reason, no reason at all. Look at me. Look at my leg. I'm going to be lame for a long while, perhaps the rest of my life, and you talk about difficulties. My wife and children have had to leave town, and you——"

A nurse came hurrying in. I must have been yelling louder than I realized. Koleski picked up his hat and started to slide toward the door.

"You listen to me," I said, fighting off the nurse. "If you don't find them, I will. I will if it takes me from now on. And when I do I'll make 'em wish they'd never been born."

Koleski said, "Yes, sir." He got out. The nurse pushed me down and I lay there and shook and sweated with fury. Koleski was right and I knew it, and it did not make things any easier.

And Tracey was in Boston. Everybody came to see me, Mae and my brother-in-law Vince, my parents-in-law—my own were dead—fellows from the office, secretaries from the office, friends, neighbors. They brought me stuff and told me the house was all right, and Vince kept the lawn cut, and the boss himself stopped by and told me not to worry about my job. But Tracey was in Boston and she stayed there.

The first day they let me have a phone in the room I called her. It wasn't until I heard her voice that I really understood how much I wanted her with me. She was laughing and crying and talking a blue streak all at once on the other end of the line, telling Bets over and over, "It's Daddy, it's Daddy and he's all better." Then Bets said hello and told me there was a big storm coming outside, and Tracey said, "Here's Pudge, too. Pudge, say hello to Daddy." Pudge squealed and made breathy gurgling sounds.

"Tracey," I said. "Tracey——"

"Oh, Walt, you don't know how dreadful it's been. Getting that call and going down to the hospital in the middle of the night, seeing you like that, not knowing whether you were going to live or die—— And then that letter. It's been like a terrible nightmare."

"I know. But, Tracey——"

"The last thing on earth I wanted to do was go away, I felt as though I was deserting you, and yet there didn't seem to be anything else to do. They threatened to hurt the children, and I just couldn't take any chances, Walt. I just couldn't."

"Of course not. What did it say, exactly? The letter."

"Oh, horrible things. Nobody was to try and find out who they were or they would get the children. I was to burn the letter, not show it to anybody. I think that detective was angry with me, but I was afraid, without you there to help me."

"Sure. Listen, Tracey, can you remember the postmark, what kind of paper it was written on, anything about it that——"

"No. I was absolutely terrified, Walt, there all alone with the children, not knowing what was going to happen. Perhaps I wasn't thinking very straight, but I don't see how anybody could have expected me to."

"But can't you remember——"

"Walt, I've been all through this with the police, and I don't know any more than I did then. I'm so happy to hear your voice, darling, let's talk about that. How do you feel?"

We talked about that. I was very cheerful. Then I said, "When are you coming home?"

There was a short but perfectly apparent silence.

"Why," she said, "just as soon as it's safe."

"What do you mean, safe?"

"When they've caught those people. Why, Walt, you don't mean that you want me to stay all alone out there with the children, and you in the hospital, and those men——"

"Boys," I said. "Anyway, you don't have to bring the kids. Leave them there for a while. You can stay with your folks."

"Auntie isn't well. She couldn't possibly take care of——"

"Well, get a nursemaid, then."

"Walt, I'm doing the best I know how, and it hasn't been easy at all, it's been terrible. Don't make it any harder for me." She began to cry. "Why did all this have to happen? What did we do to deserve it? And what kind of a town is it where the police let things like that go on?" She finished on a note of hysteria. "I don't think I ever want to go back to Mall's Ford!"

"I'm afraid you're going to have to," I told her.

Again there was a silence on the line.

"Well," she said, after a minute, "of course. I didn't really mean that. As soon as it's safe——"

"Sooner than that," I said. "They'll be sending me home one of these days. I've got to have a home to go to and somebody to look after me. I'm afraid that's your job, Tracey. You're my wife."

"Yes, Walt," she whispered. "Yes. I know."

She hung up. I shut my eyes and remembered, and there was a lot to remember, from the first time I met her. It had been good. We'd been happy. I could remember Tracey a hundred ways but somehow I could not picture this person I had just talked to in Boston. I tried and tried, but somehow it would not come out like Tracey.

I opened my eyes again, and Mae was there.

"I just talked to Tracey," I said.

"Fine," said Mae, all smiles. "When is she coming back?"

"She's still frightened. Mae, did she show you that letter?"

"Why, no, Walt. No, she didn't."

"Did she show it to anybody?"

"She might have. I don't know." She went to the window. "My, it's a lovely day. I'd have brought you more lilacs for the room, but they're——"

"Don't change the subject. What happened those nine days I was unconscious? What did Tracey do?"

"Just what I told you. She waited until you were out of danger and then she took the children to Boston."

"Out of danger," I said. "You mean by that they knew I was going to live, but they weren't sure how."

"You were a pretty sick boy."

My head still ached when I tried hard to think, but this was something I had to know.

"I might have had some permanent damage to the brain, something that would have made me——"

25

"Well, you didn't, Walt, thank the Lord. You're all right. Let's just be grateful for that."

"But I might have. No, don't try to steer me off. You don't think there really was any letter, do you?"

"You're getting upset," she said. "I'd better go."

"Answer me, Mae."

She looked at the floor, out the window, anywhere but at me. "I can't. I don't know. Don't ask me, Walt."

"I'm asking you. You don't believe there ever was a letter, do you?"

Now she did look at me, her eyes bright and blazing. "Let me ask you something. What did you marry Tracey for?"

"Because I love her. Because she's pretty and gay and a lot of fun."

"All right, then. Why blame her for being what she is?"

It took a minute for that to sink in. Then I said, finding it hard to speak, "You women sure hang together."

"It isn't my place to talk about your wife," said Mae furiously. "But if you insist on it, I will. She ran out on you. If you'd died she could have stood it, but when it looked as though you might be left helpless on her hands to take care of, she ran. That's what I think. That's what her parents think, too. No, I don't believe there ever was a letter. Now are you satisfied?"

I didn't answer that. After a while I said, "She doesn't have that reason now. If she isn't frightened, what's holding her back?"

"If it was me," said Mae, "I wouldn't be in any hurry to look you in the face again."

There was another one of those painful pauses. I seemed to be experiencing a lot of them these days.

"We're probably all wrong," she said impulsively. "Give her a chance, Walt. After all, it is the first time life ever reared up and kicked her. It must have been a dreadful shock."

I said, "Yes. It must have been. Have you seen Obermeyer?"

"Not today. Why?"

"I want to know how soon I can get out of here."

She looked at me narrowly. "What's all the sudden hurry?"

"I've got something to do."

"Walt, are you crazy? You leave that to the police."

26

"Police," I said. "Ha."

"That's unfair. Koleski's doing everything he can. They can't just pick people out of thin air."

"This didn't happen to Koleski. It happened to me. I've got a special interest."

"You forget it. If you want to know about that letter, you ask Tracey."

"Do you think she's likely to admit she made it up?"

"I don't know," said Mae, "but I know what happened to you the last meeting you had with those boys. I don't think you could stand another one."

I thought probably she was right. But at that particular moment I didn't care.

From now on, no matter what Tracey did, there would be a wall between us until I got the truth about that letter.

That was on a Tuesday. On Thursday, Tracey came back. She walked in unheralded, as fresh and pretty as a bunch of roses, and she kissed me and put her arms around me and cried, and it was just as though there had never been a question between us, or a second's doubt. Nothing had changed, nothing was any different, except that there was a little line now at each end of Tracey's mouth, very faint, almost invisible from being so new, but quite hard, quite set. I noticed, too, that it was difficult to catch her eye. It got to be a game, trying to make her look straight at me. I played it all the time she was there. I lost.

I didn't say anything to her. I didn't have so much pride that I could afford to throw it around and somehow I didn't want to bring up the whole subject, anyway. If she had been telling the truth, I didn't want to be the one to accuse her unjustly. If she hadn't, I couldn't prove it. Not now. That would come later. Much later, when I wasn't so sore and bruised inside, when I was better used to the idea and wouldn't mind seeing her forced out all shamed and naked from behind her sheltering pretenses.

Pretty and gay and a lot of fun. Mae was right. This sort of thing didn't give Tracey much scope for her particular talents. She looked at the rig they had on my leg, with the toes sticking up out of it, puffy and bluish, and then she went and stood by the open window, taking deep breaths.

"I'll get better," I told her. Suddenly I wanted to laugh, not because anything was very funny, but because she looked sicker than I did, and I felt I had to cheer her up.

"They're going to take more X-rays Monday. If they look good they'll put another gismo on it and then maybe I can go home."

"That's wonderful."

"I'm damned sick of this place, I can tell you."

"I'll have everything ready. Without the children there to bother you, you can get a good rest."

The last thing I planned to do was rest, but I didn't argue.

Then she asked me if I had seen Mr. Koleski lately.

"He dropped by yesterday," I said.

"Has he found those boys yet?"

"No."

Do you want them caught, I wondered, so that your children will be safe? Or do you not want them caught, because they will deny your story?

Her face was turned partly away from me. I couldn't read it.

"I suppose he is trying," she said. "But it does seem terrible if people can do a thing like that and get away with it."

"Tracey," I said, "you get around the neighborhood more than I do. Do you know a tall skinny boy named Bill?"

She looked puzzled until I explained. Then she bent her head and frowned, as though she was trying hard to think. Finally she said, "No, I don't."

"He's the key," I said. "If we could find him we could find the others."

"Who is we?" said Tracey. "The only business you have now is to get well."

I didn't argue that, either.

"Walt."

"Yes?" She had her back to me now, full on, looking out the window at the sooty mill sheds. It was one of those north-wind days when spring goes gray and cheerless, and there was not even the Bessemer to liven the view.

"Father came up to Boston. He seemed to think I was trying to——" She hesitated, choosing her words. "He practically accused me of trying to evade my responsibilities."

That was interesting news, but I made no comment.

She asked me point-blank, "Is that what you think?"

Attack, I thought, is always the best defense. I looked at her. She had taken her hat off, and her hair was fleecy bright around her head like a Botticelli angel. Her back was slim and her hips were just nicely rounded, and her ankles were fine-turned and graceful. She was lovely. She was Tracey. She was my wife, and we had had children together and laughed together and been happy. I wanted to take her in my arms and tell her of course I didn't think any such thing, and I wanted to mean it.

I said, "You did what you had to."

She stood by the window for a long time. "Yes," she said at last. "I did."

The nurse came in to tell us visiting time was up. Tracey turned around and smiled and kissed me, and I kissed her, and we made the customary jokes with the nurse, and then she left, and I lay there feeling like hell. Donne said that no man is an island. He was wrong. Every living thing is an island, and sometimes our shores touch, but that's all. The inner country remains inviolate and inviolable, no matter how much we may want to open it up. And this is a damned lonely thing.

I pretended to go to sleep, and after the nurse went out I watched the gray day darken outside the window and the darkness got into me too. I thought of five boys and what their act of casual violence had cost me. I thought of what I was going to do to make them pay for it. I got a new clear feeling in me, not a pleasant one, but very strong. I got a new taste in my mouth. The bitter, stimulating taste of vengeance, not here yet but surely coming.

4

I⊤ must have been six or seven weeks later when I dropped in on Koleski in the big dingy gray-stone building that houses the Mall's Ford Police Department. I know it was one of the first times I was out by myself without Tracey to drive me. They had taken the cast off my leg and put a brace on it instead, and the orthopedics man was very happy. The knee was responding better than he had hoped, and he figured that in two or three years, with the right care, there wouldn't be a thing the matter with it. This made me happy too. It made me so happy that I limped into a bar across the street from the hospital and had two double whiskies to keep from laughing till I cried. But I could get around now. And the first place I went was Koleski's office.

Other matters, I suppose, had come up in the meantime, because for a second or two he was a little vague about the case. But he gave me a chair and a cigarette and warm handshake, and after that the bad news.

"I'm afraid it's a dead end for the present, Mr. Sherris. We haven't turned up a thing."

"'For the present,'" I repeated. "Then I take it the case is still alive."

"A case is always alive until we make the arrest. Do you know anything about crime detection?"

"About as much as the average layman, I suppose."

"Well," said Koleski, "you probably know that a hit-and-run deal like this is the hardest of all to pin down. There's nothing to go on. Unless you get a break like a license number or a positive identification, something really definite, you just have to wait until the criminal makes a mistake, or somebody talks too much. Usually, with juveniles, that isn't too long."

"It sounds pretty indefinite to me."

Koleski shrugged, with just a shade of annoyance. "Tell us who the boy named Bill is, and we can have the bunch of them in five minutes."

"That's a funny thing," I said. "I've beaten my brains out trying to think. Bill is a common enough name and tall skinny boys come in job lots, but I can't find him. If the shape is right, the name is wrong, and vice versa. I've worn my wife to a shadow, driving me around. The service station, the supermarket, neighbors I never saw before. I've checked everything I could think of. Nothing."

"Then you have some idea of what we're up against."

"Yes," I said. "I have. But there's one difference. You can go home and forget about it. I can't."

He said earnestly, "Don't let this become an obsession with you, Mr. Sherris."

"That's what my wife's been telling me. But I wonder. Maybe somebody ought to be obsessed. Look at these."

I took two newspaper clippings from my pocket and laid them on his desk. They were small clippings, these little three- or four-line fillers you find at the bottom of a column on days when there was a half inch of space left over and nothing better to put into it. Koleski read them, frowning. Then he put them down again neatly, side by side, and shook his head.

"People like this, Mr. Sherris—transients and can-gangers— are always getting into trouble."

"But not this kind of trouble. These weren't ordinary brawls. These were beatings, where the victim was all by himself and was suddenly set upon for no reason, and by nobody he knew. I'd like to know if there were more cases like this, ones that never did make the paper. I'd like to know exactly what the victims said."

He looked at me as though he was now convinced that I had gone queer on the subject of beatings.

"Listen," I told him. "Take me. They thought I was a tramp prowling in a dark lonely place. Now suppose they decided they liked that kind of work and wanted to do more of it? Who do you

31

think they'd pick for their victims? And you know what happens, sooner or later."

"What?"

"Somebody gets accidentally hit too hard and you have a murder on your hands. Or perhaps it's the other way round. One of the victims defends himself with a knife, or perhaps he has a gun. Either way——"

He sighed. "All right," he said. "I'll get the files."

He was gone for a while. When he came back he had a batch of folders.

"These are all the assault cases for which no arrests have been made, dating from April seventeenth. That was the night they got you."

"Yes," I said. "I remember."

We began to go through the typed reports. Most of them were the usual thing and of no interest to me. There were several cases involving a gang of boys, but Koleski said Juvenile Division had a line on them, they thought, and they weren't mine. I agreed, because the cases were all purse snatchings, and the victims, all women, had been slugged merely in the line of business.

We wound up with four. Two of them were the full reports of the cases mentioned in the clippings. The other two were identical except in detail.

"You're the detective," I said, "and I'm not trying to tell you your business. But look at these." I shoved the folders at him. "Here are four men. Two of them are transients—to put it more crudely—tramps. Two are members of the local can-gang, which comes to about the same thing. Each one of them was savagely beaten up by persons unknown, in a place where there were no witnesses and at a time when the victim was too drunk to defend himself, or to remember clearly what happened. There was, of course, no question of robbery involved. Now look at the dates. With me as the starting point, it figures out at roughly one every three weeks. That's an awful lot of unprovoked assaults even for that stratum of society, isn't it?"

Koleski looked genuinely thoughtful. "It's hard to say. A lot of things happen in the jungle that we don't ever hear about. Also, these guys don't like cops. They don't tell a straight story.

They don't want to get mixed up with the law and if they are pulled in for questioning they just play dumb. Sometimes they don't even know their own names."

He turned the typewritten pages over.

"Three of them are unable to say how many attacked them. The fourth refers to his assailants as 'a couple of guys.' If it was the same group each time, and I'll admit there's a similarity in these cases, all right, it still doesn't sound like your five boys."

"It was dark, and the man was blind drunk. He wouldn't know the difference."

"Even a drunk, Mr. Sherris, usually knows whether it was one guy or five that hit him. And I wouldn't depend too much on these statements that the attackers were unknown. The victims would say that in any case. They don't pull the law into their private quarrels."

I said, "Then you don't think it would be any use to question these men again."

"No use in the world. Matter of fact, it isn't even possible with at least two of them. The nonresidents were sent on their way as undesirables as soon as they were discharged from the hospital."

"You could pick up the other two. Just for questioning."

"Look, Mr. Sherris. You just said you weren't trying to tell me my business." He leaned forward in an attitude of pleading. "We're a hard-working police department, no matter what anybody says. We're shorthanded. Vacations, an epidemic of summer flu, and two patrolmen in the hospital with gunshot wounds incurred in the line of duty. We have a murder case on our hands and two major robberies. Please. Be reasonable."

I got up. "I've written down the names, anyway. You don't mind that, do you?"

"I can't stop you from doing what you want to on your own. But I'm telling you, Mr. Sherris, you'd do much better to leave this entirely to us."

"You mean you don't want any amateur assistance."

"I mean you were lucky once," he said. "Don't count on it twice. We'll get them. It may take us a while. But we'll get them."

"I'm sure you will," I said. "Thanks anyway."

I left him looking worried and went back to the parking lot to get my car. It was a stinking-hot afternoon with an ugly blue-blackness building up in the west. My shirt stuck to my back, and the brace chafed and my leg ached, and I felt low and mean as a rattlesnake crawling down that blistering stretch of sidewalk, leaning like an old man on a cane.

I got into the car and drove to Beekman Street and parked in the middle of the block. I could see the sign of Noddy's bar and grille ahead. Behind me, around the corner on East Federal, was the number given as the residence of one Harold Francis, the victim of the most recent of the four beatings.

I hesitated a minute on the sidewalk and then I turned up to Federal. The pavement was dirty and so were the building fronts and the pawnshops, the barrooms and the ill-smelling markets and the people. Little knots of men with unshaven chins and ragged pants leaned against the buildings and watched me go by. I had on a clean shirt, clean that morning, anyway. I felt overdressed and uncomfortable, the target of every eye.

I passed the decent windows of the Welfare Industries show-room and found the number I was looking for, a grimy doorway with a glass bulb hung out over it. The bulb said HOTEL. Inside was a hall so badly lighted you couldn't see the dirt, you could only smell it. There was a desk there, and a big shaggy man behind it. I asked him about Harold Francis.

He looked at me and my clean shirt with the cold hostility of a man looking at an enemy.

"Who?"

I repeated the name. "He gave this as his address. I'm not a cop. There's no trouble. I'd just like to talk to him."

"He moved."

"Where?"

"How should I know? He got in some kind of a beef, I ain't seen him since. I don't keep track, mister."

"Would you know anyone who could tell me? A friend of his, maybe?"

"No."

And that was that. I gave up finally and went back down the

street to Noddy's. The corner of Beekman and Front had an international flavor, all right. There was a Greek coffeehouse, a Spanish restaurant, a Puerto Rican restaurant, an Italian food importer, and some kind of a Syrian lodge with a sign in Arabic. The block running east seemed to be solid Negro, full of women sitting in the hot doorways and little brown children playing on the pavement. That block dead-ended against a high black wall, and beyond the wall was my old friend the Bessemer, going like a Roman candle fifty feet high in a showering glory of burning flakes, sending up a plume of reddish smoke. Thunder muttered distantly in the west. I went into Noddy's and sat down on a stool at the bar.

It was cooler in there, but the air was dead and stale, moving heavily where the blades of two big ceiling fans pushed it. Four couples sat at tables and there were several men at the bar. A juke box was banging away. Otherwise the place was reasonably quiet, and clean enough to get by the health inspector. I ordered a beer. The bartender gave me a close look, and I asked him,

"Are you Noddy?"

"That's me. Bottle or draft?"

I told him draft, and he brought it. He was a thick-jawed, thick-shouldered man, shrewd, intelligent, and tough as a ten-penny spike. I liked him. He'd been able to make out and do well in a world where I wouldn't have lasted five minutes.

"My name is Sherris," I said. "Last April you had trouble with some boys who came in here and raised a row because you wouldn't serve them."

"I didn't, either," he said. "Who are you?"

"Nobody from the Liquor Control Board." I told him who I was. He looked sympathetic but he shook his head.

"I already talked to the cops about that. I don't know anything more than I said. But I'll tell you, mister. They blame all this juvenile-delinquency stuff and like that onto the poor slum kids, but you never hear about what these young punks from uptown get away with. You know why? Because their fathers pay off their fines, and their mothers bawl, and the judge, he thinks these are real nice people, let's give 'em another chance. Hah!"

"Look," I said, "isn't there some little thing you could remember about them, something you didn't tell Koleski? Just a stray word, maybe, anything that might give a hint what part of town they came from, where they went to school."

Noddy thought hard. "Nope. Nothing. The other four didn't say too much. They let the big one do the talking. He was a dandy."

"Yes," I said. "And strong, too."

"Good-looking kid, if he wasn't so snotty. Real handsome, you know? Smart, too. I wish my own boy was half as smart. But"—Noddy made a gesture of pushing away—"no good. Too smart, maybe. You know? Sometimes too smart is worse than being a little dumb."

"What about the tall skinny one?" I asked. "Can you tell me anything about him?"

"No. I remember there was one of 'em, though—sawed-off type, didn't look too bright—he had a laugh on him like a jackass."

"I know," I said. I drank my beer, feeling baffled and depressed. So far I hadn't got anything but hot and tired. Noddy moved off to serve another customer. The fans whirred. One of the women at the tables burst with the regularity of a metronome into shrill laughter. Down the bar one of the men regretfully finished his beer, practically squeezing the glass to get the last drop out of it, and then he turned and walked out the door with even, careful steps looking straight ahead. He was not drunk but he would not ever be really sober again, either. And he gave me an idea.

I got out the paper with the four names and the two addresses written on it. I waited till Noddy came back, and I showed it to him.

"Would you happen to know any of these men?"

His face became as blank as a shuttered window. "Lots of guys come in here. I don't know the half of 'em."

"Tell you what," I said. "If you should happen to run across any of them, tell them I'd like to talk to them." I explained why.

Noddy looked at me suspiciously. "Why don't you hunt 'em up yourself?"

"I tried. And I got just what you're giving me now." I put one of my business cards on top of the piece of paper. "Tell 'em there's money in it. And I promise not to get anyone into trouble. They wouldn't believe me if I told them that. They might believe you."

I went out, giving him no chance to shove the paper back at me. I didn't know whether anything would come of it or not. Probably not. Probably Koleski was right. Anyway, it was a try.

The storm had moved closer, and it was dead still and hot as the inside of a furnace. I crawled back to my car and drove homeward by way of Williams Avenue.

I passed the plant. They would not hold my job for me forever, and Tracey was beginning to worry out loud about the money. I thought of how much those five boys had cost me in dollars and cents, over and above insurance. I wanted to go back to work as a return to normalcy, to the life I had been living before this happened. Yet I didn't want to because there was a gnawing restlessness on me to hunt these nameless shadows, to track them down and force them into the light. The police would keep the case open, but already more urgent things had taken their attention. It might be years before the boys were caught. It might be never.

I passed the place where it happened.

A wave of physical sickness came over me. I hung onto the wheel and I thought, I've got to find them, I will find them. Then the thunder rumbled and the rain began to fall, blowing cold on my face, and I knew that I would not find them, that they were safe behind the darkness and the namelessness, safe to maul and tear as the whim took them, young tigers roaming in the forest of the night.

And there was still the question of the letter.

They had cost me more than money, more than time or pain or health. They had cost me my faith in Tracey. And they were going to get away with it.

Why?

Why should they be allowed to get away with it? Why should they have the right to do what they did and have it all forgotten? Koleski can forget. All the people who read about it in the paper and shook their heads and clucked their tongues against their teeth, they can forget. Only I can't forget. I was the victim.

Rain drummed on the top of the car. It was dark with that slaty storm-darkness, and thunder cracked and boomed, and lightning made a lurid flaring in the gloom. I was out of town, on the tree-lined road that serves the Northside suburbs. The rain fell in sheets, clogging the windshield wipers. I slowed and turned on my parking lights. And a light-colored convertible went around me like the wind, throwing out a great contemptuous wave of spray.

A gray convertible with a black top and white side-wall tires, a souped-up job with twin tail pipes, roaring as it went.

It raced away from me down the narrow shining road, under the trees and the storm-shadow and the pouring rain. This is the way they were headed that night, I thought. Williams Avenue feeds this road, and they were coming from town, not toward it. They live out here somewhere, not far away from me, and they use this road, and that looks like the same car. Something tightened inside my head.

The same car. Their car.

I jammed the throttle down to the floor.

My tires whined and sang against the wet road. I took the curves wide and fast but I wasn't afraid or excited and my car was under perfect control. There were others on the road but they didn't matter, they flicked past and were gone. I kept my eyes on the gray blur ahead of me, following it like a star. I could hear the sound of its motor under all the noise of wind and thunder. It sounded just as it had that night when it stopped in front of me on Williams Avenue.

Their car.

It came closer. Suddenly I was on top of it. Through the glass of the back curtain I could see heads inside, dark shapeless blobs in the gloom and the rain-blur, and one of them turned a white surface toward me as though in startled fright. I smiled and leaned on the horn. The spray flew up from the puddles on either side and we raced together, the convertible and I, under the wind-lashed trees.

A red light blinked ahead in the murk. We were coming up

on a main intersection. The convertible put on a sudden burst of speed. I settled myself behind the wheel. There was a dead service station on the corner, one of these old one-pump affairs in front of a shacky store, and it had been closed for a long time. I thought I knew what the convertible was going to do.

It did. It angled off into the station yard, churning up mud and gravel, rocking from side to side. I was supposed to go straight through, unable to stop. But I didn't. I stood the car on its nose, let up again, and spun around the turn on two wheels. The convertible came to a stop not three feet away and I had them boxed. I had them cornered.

I took my heavy cane in my hand and got out and went over to the gray car, with a curious flicker of light before my eyes and a tight pain in my head.

I pulled open the door.

5

THERE must have been a period of five or six seconds—it couldn't have been much longer—when I stood looking into the car, and they sat looking out, and nothing happened. Then, almost simultaneously, they began to scream. They were not boys at all. They were girls. Two girls, side by side in the front seat. I had never seen either of them before.

All of a sudden the rain had turned cold and drenching and there was no excitement any more. I let go of the door and stepped back.

The girl in the driver's seat shrieked, "Don't you touch us!" The other one flung herself at the opposite door. I kept backing away, trying to say something, but they were both scrambling out of the car now. They began to run around, yelling for help.

There was a produce stand across the road on one corner and a diner on the other. People were already staring out of both of them to see what the trouble was. A couple of cars were slowing down. One pulled in next to mine and three hardy-looking millworkers got out. The girls flew to them, sobbing, pointing at me.

I opened the door of my own car, the off-side door, being the nearest, and sat down with my feet still out in the rain. All I could think of was that gray convertible flying down the road with me after it. I saw it go off the road in forty different ways. I saw those wretched girls dead, dying, dismembered, maimed, and all because of me. It could so easily have happened. It was a miracle that it hadn't happened. I looked once more at the convertible to make sure. Then put my head in my hands and just sat there, shaking.

"Drunk, huh?" said one of the millworkers, with rough disgust. He reached in and took my keys. "You're not going any place, Mac."

I told him I wasn't even going to try.

A crowd was gathering in spite of the rain. The three millworkers appointed themselves my guards, and some other people wrapped raincoats around the girls and took them over to the diner. We were all waiting for the cops. Somebody had called them, of course. It crossed my mind that Tracey would have words to say if she found out about this, and that I had put an ideal weapon into her hands to use against me. But at that particular moment I didn't care. I didn't care about anything except that there hadn't been an accident.

The storm went on its way, and the downpour slackened to a chilly drizzle. I wanted to put on my jacket, but one of my guards had to make sure first that there was no gun in the pocket.

"Your kind," he said, "can't be trusted. Okay." He threw the jacket at me. "Put it on."

"What do you mean," I asked him, "my kind?"

"Goddamn rapist, that's what I mean. What do you think I mean? Those poor little girls——"

"Oh Lord," I said. "It wasn't like that at all. I thought——" I looked at their three hard unsympathetic faces and gave up. They wouldn't have believed anything I said.

About two minutes before the police car came, it occurred to me that convertible still might be the right car, that the boy who owned it could perfectly well have a sister, or sisters. I wished I could ask the girls but I didn't think I could make the men understand that, either. I didn't try.

The police came. There were two of them in the car. One of them went over to talk to the girls and the other one questioned me. The three mill hands hung over his shoulder and listened while I tried to explain.

"Don't believe a word of it," one of them said to the cop. "He's nothing but a goddamned rapist. I saw him with my own eyes, chasing those poor little girls——"

"With that?" I said, pointing to the brace on my leg. "And

41

if I was going to commit rape I wouldn't pick a gravel patch on a main crossroads, in a pouring rain." I said to the cop, "You don't have to take my word for it. Ask Detective Koleski."

He said he would. The other cop came back with the girls. They got in the convertible and drove away, giving me dirty looks. I didn't blame them. The two cops talked for a minute, and then the one who had questioned me retrieved my keys, handed them to me, and motioned me under the wheel. He got in beside me.

"Downtown," he said.

I drove downtown with the police car hanging on my bumper.

"Who did you say knew you?" the cop asked once. It was the only time he spoke.

I told him again. "Detective Koleski. I was talking to him just a couple of hours ago."

And how I wished I had taken his advice. Of all the people I could think of in the world, City Detective Peter Koleski was the last one I wanted to see. But I drove on slowly and carefully, and the rain stopped and the sun came out again, pretty well down now and considerably subdued, and then there I was back again at Police Headquarters.

They made me wait while one of them went up and talked to Koleski. After a few minutes Koleski phoned to have me come up too. The cop who had questioned me said,

"All right, mister, he backs up your story, and if he can get you off the hook with those girls it's all right with me. But I'm warning you——"

"You don't need to. I feel lousy enough already. If anything had happened——"

"You just hold to that thought," said Koleski angrily. "It may keep you from doing some other damn-fool thing in the future. Okay, boys, I'll take it from here."

The cops went away and Koleski sat down at his desk.

"Look," I said. "I——"

"Shut up," he said. "I'm going to try and get you out of this."

He looked at a paper one of the cops had given him, picked up the phone and asked for a number. He got it. He must have talked for half an hour while I sat, dumped and ashamed and miserable, and listened. At first the party on the other end did all the talking. I could hear a woman's voice going like fury, and all Koleski said was, "Yes, Mrs. Wosnicek. I understand, Mrs. Wosnicek. No, Mrs. Wosnicek." But somehow, imperceptibly, it swung the other way, and by the time he was finished it was Mrs. Wosnicek who was doing the yes-and-no bit, as one warmly, even eagerly, co-operating with the police. Finally Koleski thanked her for her invaluable help and hung up. Then he glared at me.

I didn't say anything. When he was through glaring he read to me, without comment, from the notes he had been scribbling while he talked.

"The convertible is registered in the name of Howard Wosnicek. Howard Wosnicek is the brother of Gloria Wosnicek, who was driving the car this afternoon. Howard is at present serving his country in the United States Navy. He has been doing so for nearly two years, and on April seventeenth last he was on a tour of duty in the Canal Zone. I have explained to Mrs. Wosnicek——"

"I heard you."

"Well, you didn't seem to hear me very well this afternoon, Sherris, so I wanted to make sure. You hear me now? Then listen. You've got a greivance. It's a legitimate grievance. But it doesn't give you any special rights. It doesn't suspend any laws. You're still required to behave yourself as a responsible citizen. If you don't, you'll wind up downstairs in a cell just as fast, or faster, than the boys you're looking for. Is that understood?"

"Don't worry. I've had my lesson."

"I hope so. Where'd you go after you left here this afternoon? Before the convertible, I mean."

"To Noddy's. It didn't come to anything."

"Well, take it easy on the way home. And Sherris——"

"What?"

"We'll get 'em."

I went out and got in the car and drove homeward again. This time I made it.

Tracey met me at the door. "Where have you been all this time? I was getting worried."

43

"Just around," I said. Bets came running up, and I sat down on the couch and took her on my lap. "Get me a drink, will you, Tracey? I'm beat."

She went into the kitchen, still talking to me. "What do you mean, around? You must have gone somewhere that took so long."

I told her I had been to see Koleski and the bartender.

"Did you learn anything?"

"No."

Bets snuggled up under my jacket, butting her head against me to make me pet her, in a puppyish way she has. "Daddy's all wet," she said. "Daddy went out in the rain." She was feeling my shirt, which was still damp. Pudge was in his playpen across the room, and this seemed to strike him as funny because he let out a hoarse squeal of laughter and pounded the corner post with his fat fists. The youngsters had been home for a little over three weeks now. So far nobody had threatened them, and by some unspoken consent Tracey and I had not discussed the possibility. When I got well enough the kids came home, and that was it.

Tracey returned with a highball, which she put in my hand, and then she bent over Pudge, who held up his arms to be lifted.

"Come on, doll-baby. Time for bed."

"Ooh," said Bets. "Daddy's cold."

The ice cubes were clattering in the glass. I set it down. Tracey turned around with Pudge in her arms. Her face was alarmed. I put Bets on the couch and tried hard to stop shaking.

"I had a little trouble with the car," I said. "In the rain. I guess I got wet."

I wasn't cold at all but I was ashamed to tell her the truth. She put Pudge back in the pen and left him bawling there, and sent Bets for dry towels, and made me go in the bedroom and take off my shirt. Then she scrubbed me with the towels until I was crimson, lecturing me the way she does the kids.

I caught her hands and held her. "You've been good to me these last weeks."

Her face became subtly altered and her eyes avoided mine. "I'm your wife, Walt."

"I know, but you have been good, beyond the call of duty. Patient, too, even when I was acting like a skunk."

She tried to draw her hands away. "You'll get cold again. I'll get you a dry shirt——"

"And a drink," I said. "A straight one this time."

I let her go. Between lovers, things don't need to be said. Between strangers, there isn't any way you can say them.

I put on the shirt and drank the drink. We smiled and ate our dinner and put the kids to bed and pretended to be a family.

I dreamed a lot that night. Mostly I chased that damned convertible down a dark wet road, and wrecked it, and picked the bodies out of a ditch. But every once in a while I could hear Chuck's voice speaking to me, laughing, saying, "We even took your wife away, and you'll never find us." And I would try to find him in the dark but I never could.

The next afternoon the whole story of the convertible was in the paper, a neat little item right on the front page, naming names, times, and places. One of the reporters on the regular police beat got it, I suppose, or else somebody who knew somebody on the paper happened to be there, I don't know. But they ran it. Victim of Beating Chases Wrong Car, occupants narrowly escape accident. And so on.

Tracey read it. "I can understand," she said, "why you didn't want to tell me about it."

I was angry for the obvious reasons and the old, not-so-obvious reasons. I said, "I guess we've all done things we'd rather not have shouted from the housetops."

"What do you mean by that?"

"Just exactly what I said." Which was no answer, but I wasn't going to let her bait me out into an open accusation where she could really let go at me. "Anyway, it's all right for you and Koleski to be perfectly calm and reasonable. Suppose you were me, and you were sure it was the same car. What would you have done?"

"I guess you couldn't help it," she said in a curiously subdued voice. "But you know what it means."

All of a sudden she jumped up and caught Pudge in her arms protectively, and turned on me.

"Those boys will read it in the paper. They'll know you're

trying to find them and they might do anything, Walt. Anything."

"Yes," I said. "They'll probably laugh themselves right into hysterics with sheer fright."

"All right," she said. "Make a joke of it. But if anything happens to the children I'll never forgive you."

She ran past me into the house—we'd been sitting on the terrace, trying to find a breeze—still carrying Pudge. The exit line and the exit itself seemed pure theatrics to me. But then I looked at Bets playing hide-and-seek with the cat in the middle of the best flower bed, and I thought how diabolically clever Tracey had been to hang her lie on that particular peg. Because you didn't dare to assume wholeheartedly that it was a lie. You didn't dare.

And then I realized two things. I realized the flaw in Tracey's cleverness and what I had to do about it.

The flaw was simply that the danger was so great that you couldn't live with it. If your wife and children had by the remotest chance been threatened by a gang of hoodlums, you had to remove that threat. Beside the possibility of harm to them, the possibility of your wife having made up the whole thing to get herself out of a situation she didn't have guts enough to face was relatively unimportant.

What I had to do about it, of course, was the same thing I had wanted to do all along. Catch the boys.

But I couldn't go blundering around any longer acting on impulse, embarrassing Koleski who was doing his best to help me, getting myself in jams and making the possible danger to Tracey and the kids even greater.

I had to start on some new plan of attack, something with a modicum of brains behind it.

I sat there for a while, thinking. It was hot, not quite as bad as yesterday but bad enough. Bets laughed and scrambled around, but otherwise it was quiet.

Then all of a sudden a car came screaming up the street.

6

Our house is set well back on a graded lot and a thick planting of shrubbery screens the suburban drive. I couldn't see the car. I could only hear it, but the sweat broke out on me and I yelled, "Bets! Bets!", getting up out of my chair and going toward her as fast as I could.

She looked at me, startled. I heard Tracey come out of the house behind me, and then the car roared up around where the drive bends into the beginning of a series of sweeping curves that wind all through the subdivision. Now I could see it.

It was a black car. The driver was a young fellow who lived somewhere up the road. I knew him well by sight. He was going too damned fast, but that was all.

I waited until I got my breath back, calming Bets with a story about a big bee which had now gone away. Then I went back to the terrace. Tracey was still standing there, with an expression of fright on her white face that could not possibly have been faked.

"What is it?" she asked. "What happened?"

She could be telling the truth, I thought. Mae says she lied, and her parents think she did, and I—don't know. But she could be telling the truth.

"Sit down," I said. "I want to talk to you."

She wouldn't sit down until I had explained about the speeding car and how I had been mistaken and everything was all right. Then she perched on the edge of a chair, her head poised in such a way that she could watch both Bets and me. Her hands moved nervously in her lap.

"What is it, Walt?"

"I want you to take the kids and go away for a week or two. Now, I mean. This afternoon."

She stared at me. "But——"

"You've had a hard couple of months and you could use a rest. Go up the lake. The kids would love it."

She shook her head stubbornly. "Come right out and say it. Say what you mean."

"Well, you've already said it. If those boys do decide to drop around, I don't want any of you here."

She sat perfectly still, not saying anything, not looking at me, her mind running fast behind her eyes. Suddenly I felt sorry for her. She looked so little and so tired, caught in a web that kept catching her and tripping her when she least expected it. Suddenly I didn't care if she had lied and been frightened and run away. She was Tracey and I loved her. I wanted her safe.

"Go on, honey," I said. "Pack your things. I'll call your folks and make the arrangements." They owned a cottage at the lake, and would be only too glad to have Tracey and the kids come up.

She must have sensed some new tone in my voice. Tears came into her eyes, and for a minute I thought she was going to throw herself in my arms and tell me the whole story. But she didn't.

She only said, "And what are you planning to do?"

"I have an idea or two. They may not come to much, but I don't want to have to be worried every minute about what's happening here."

"You won't let it drop, will you?" she said with an angry fierceness. "You're going to hang to it until you get yourself killed."

"When they threatened you," I said, "they didn't leave me much choice."

"Oh no," she said. "No, Walt. Don't try to tell me you're doing this to protect me or the children. You're doing it just out of sheer vengefulness."

She turned and went into the house. And there was so much truth in what she said that I couldn't argue with her.

I drove them the fifty miles to the lake, and Tracey said not a word the whole way, except to the children. She looked awful, as though she hadn't slept for a month. I thought it was time she had a rest and yet I wondered if that was what she really needed. She seemed to be fighting some inner battle with herself, drawn off small and remote in the far corner of the seat.

When we came in sight of the lake, vast and blue as the ocean, complete with boats and even a few gulls, and only lacking the sea-salt smell, Tracey said,

"Can't you forget it, Walt? Aren't these four horrible months enough to lose out of our lives?"

She turned to me with such an air of weary pleading that I almost gave in.

"Please," she said. "Stay here at the lake for a while. Get your mind on other things. You're getting so—so grim and twisted I hardly know you any more. Please, Walt. Before anything more dreadful happens."

And then I'd never know, I thought. I'd have to wonder, until the next time the going got rough, whether I have a wife or only a fair-weather friend. Somebody's got to tell me the truth. If you won't, it'll have to be Chuck.

I said aloud, "There's nothing to worry about, Tracey. I'm not going to make any more boo-boos like yesterday."

She let her head drop forward, and I thought she was going to cry. Her voice held a note of desperation.

"You're a fool. Revenge isn't worth it."

"It doesn't seem so crazy," I said, getting angry myself now, "to want a little revenge for a piece of senseless brutality like this. They'd love me to forget about it, but I'm not going to give them the satisfaction."

"All right," she said. "All right."

"Furthermore," I said, "they're still at it. They've beaten at least four other men just for the fun of it. Someday it'll be a killing."

"That's up to the police. You're no public defender."

"No, but I'm the only one with any sort of a lead to them——Oh, the devil with it! I have to do this, Tracey. Let me alone."

She let me alone. She didn't even say good-bye when I left her at the cottage. I think she knew the real reason I was being so stubborn.

Poor Tracey.

My father-in-law came out to the car with me. He fiddled around getting the last light bag out of the back, and I said, "Thanks, Dad. I'll be back in a couple of days."

"I hope so. She's terribly worried about you. I mean really worried."

"I know it," I said.

"I think," said Dad slowly, "perhaps the fault was ours. She was an only child and she grew up in a fortunate house. I think we gave her everything but maturity."

"Nobody can give you that," I said. "You've got to work for it. I'm still working. How about you?"

He shook his head and smiled briefly. He was a good guy. I was only beginning to realize how good. He said, "Take care of yourself."

"Like a rare gem. Do me a favor?"

"Of course."

"Tell her I love her. Tell her I always will."

He nodded, and I drove away.

It was after eight when I got back to Mall's Ford. I parked on Beekman Street and went into Noddy's. There was a little mob hanging around outside in the warm evening, sitting on the brick ledges under the windows or leaning against the wall, the lamp-post, the trash box, the parked cars at the curb. They weren't doing anything, just talking and laughing. Four of them were wearing pink shirts.

I went in and found an empty booth at the back. The place was pretty busy already, the juke box going full stretch at one end and television at the other. Noddy spotted me and came over. He did not look exactly hostile, but neither were his arms wide in welcome. I thought probably he had not made his mind yet what he wanted to do about those names and resented being pushed.

I hadn't come to push him and I said so. "All I want is a drink and some dinner, I'm hungry."

He said, "You didn't come to a joint like this just to eat."

"Well," I said, "I did think of something I wanted to ask you. Would you happen to know who it was the boys had the row with outside? Fellow wearing a pink shirt."

50

"Cops asked me that," he said. "I told 'em no."

"Look," I said, "I realize everybody's got their problems. I realize a lot of times there are good reasons why a perfectly innocent person would rather not get involved. But all I care about this fellow is whether he saw or heard anything that might help me."

"I'll get your drink," said Noddy. He reached over between the salt and pepper and the sugar holder and extracted a greasy card. He shoved it in my hand. "My kitchen," he said, "is cleaner than the menu. See what you want."

I took the hint and studied the menu while he went away. Somebody else brought my drink. I drank it and waited. After a while Noddy came back.

"You got prejudices?" he asked. "Jim Crow stuff?"

"Hell, no."

"Fourth booth down," he said. "I'll order for you. Guaranteed safe, I eat it myself."

I grinned. "I'm not worried," I said, lying. "Whatever he, or they, are drinking, all around, and a beer for me."

I went down to the fourth booth.

There were three men sitting in it. They were all perhaps my age or a little younger, all clean and prosperous-looking, hard-working citizens relaxing over an evening beer. One of them said, "Mr. Sherris?"

I said I was, and he motioned me to sit down. "My name's Miller. I guess I'm the one you want to talk to." He introduced me to the others, a Mr. Orris and a Mr. Page. "They were both with me that night, and they can back up what I say."

"We didn't do anything," said Orris. "They started it, right out of whole cloth. Mad because Noddy threw 'em out, I guess."

"Believe me," I said, "I'm on your side."

Miller said, "They were white boys. This isn't the South, but even so you'd just as soon not stick your neck out too far." He shook his head. "White and bad. No telling what they might say. I don't want any trouble."

"I don't think you have to worry," I said. "They're in no position to accuse anybody of anything. What did happen?"

The drinks came, and my dinner. When things were quiet again Miller said, "We were standing around outside. The three of us, some other guys, maybe eight, ten. Just standing around talking. Well, these kids came out. One of 'em a real big boy, he called me a name, with a couple of words in front of it. I guess I was in his way or something."

"That's right," said Orris, and Page nodded his head vigorously. "We weren't doing a thing."

"Now, I'll tell you, mister," said Miller. "I'm peaceable. I work hard and pay my taxes and mind my own business. But there's some certain names I just don't like to be called, especially when I'm standing on my own corner, talking to my own friends, and making no trouble for anybody. I got mad."

"We all got mad," said Page. "Wasn't just him. The whole bunch of us, and they weren't all colored, either. Couple of Spanish fellows, couple of Syrian fellows—like that. All kinds."

"Yes," said Miller. "We all got mad. They started laying their tongues on us, real dirty. I told 'em they'd better get the hell out before they got hurt, and I guess maybe I lifted my hand a little——"

Orris gave a deep throaty giggle. We all ignored it.

"Well, they ganged together like they were going to fight, but somebody behind me pulled a knife or something—I didn't see—and I guess they got the idea we were really mad. They ran like hell."

"We chased 'em some," said Page. "'Bout a block. Boy, were they making time!"

"Did they happen to say anything about where they came from or call each other by name?"

Miller shook his head. "I was so blind mad, mister, I couldn't tell you. I don't even remember what they looked like, except the big one, the one that started it. Big as a bull calf, and a real good-looking boy, too, but poison clear through."

"Yeah," said Orris. "He was the boss."

"That long skinny boy," said Page. "Him that was the first one to run. He did try to make the others shut up."

"They all looked bad to me," said Miller. "If I'd caught 'em I'd of skinned the lot."

"Almost caught one," said Orris, and chuckled again. "His foot slipped, but he kept humping on all fours like a jack rabbit. Couldn't quite snag him, and then he got going again."

"Wait a minute," said Page. "You just put me to mind of something."

"What's that?"

"Well, when the one boy was dogging it on all fours, didn't one of the others turn around and yell at him?"

"Why," said Orris, "sure he did."

They all looked at me. I didn't dare say anything. I didn't dare even hope. I had a forkful of pretty good spaghetti halfway in the air and I just froze and left it there.

"Bush," said Page triumphantly. "That's what he said. Come on, Bush!"

"Bush," I said. I put down the forkful of spaghetti. I was not hungry now. "You're sure of that. Bush."

Page said he was sure, and Orris backed him up.

"Would you know the boy again if you saw him?"

"I'd know the big boy," said Orris. "The others——" He shrugged. "Nighttime, not very good lights, things happening fast—and you know how a lot of fellows look pretty much alike. And that was four months ago."

Miller and Page said the same thing. I asked if that was all they remembered, and they said it was.

"You've been a big help," I said. "I'm grateful." I shook hands all around and got up. Noddy was at the bar. I told him what they had said. "If we do catch up with the Bush kid, could you identify him?"

He thought about it for a long minute. Then he said, "I'd like to help you. The big boy, yes. Maybe the short one with a laugh. The others—they were just—you know, boys. Nothing special to remember. After four months, I don't think I could, not to swear to it."

"But you would know the other two."

"Sure."

"Well, if we get one we'll know who the others are. Thanks a million." I put a bill on the bar for my dinner and all the beer they could handle over in the booth. Then I hiked for the car and drove to Headquarters, and all the way there that name was singing in my head.

Bush. Busch. Buesch. Bushe. Any way you spelled it, it was a lead, the first real ray of light. First names, nicknames, don't do you much good. It's a family name you need, the kind that appears in records, the kind that can be traced.

Koleski wasn't there, of course. He was on the day shift, and I suppose even a good conscientious cop has to have time out, to wash off the grime and the tears, to get a breath of air that doesn't stink of waste—the waste of lives, of youth and hope and all bright promise. I hoped he was out somewhere with a nice girl, having a good time.

I left my name and phone number with the desk sergeant, and asked to have Koleski call me as soon as he could in the morning because I had something for him. I would have liked to get things moving right that minute, but it wasn't possible, and anyway, it was only a few hours until morning. I had waited four months. I could wait a little longer.

Still up in the clouds with excitement, I found a bar and had another drink. By that time, though, I was beginning to cool off a bit, to realize what a frail little lead that name really was, and how very tough it might be to track down. I pushed that thought aside, and went out on the street again.

It was now nearly ten, but I was restless, and there was nothing to hurry home for. I thought about going to a movie. The night was pleasantly cool, and the air felt good after the stale heat in Noddy's. I went slowly up the main street, looking at the theater marquees.

After a while I realized that I didn't want to go to a movie. I wanted to go home and fall into bed. And then I realized something else.

I was afraid to go home.

I kept thinking how dark it would be there with nobody in the house to turn the yard lights on, how dark it would be under the trees and among the shrubbery, how easy for people to hide there and lie in wait.

I kept thinking about the piece in the paper telling how I had chased the wrong car, and about what Tracey had said. *They'll know you're after them and they might do anything.*

And they might. Whether they had made any formal threat to Tracey or not, they might decide to work me over again just to discourage me from looking for any more cars.

I was scared.

I could go to a hotel, I thought. But I haven't any luggage. They'd think I was drunk or crazy if I told them, Look, somebody's after me and I'm afraid to go home. They'd call the cops, and I'd be all over the papers again.

I could spend the night with Mae and Vince. They'd take me in and be glad to. Or I could drive back to the lake——

No.

Sure, they'd take you in and they'd understand why you were afraid and they wouldn't hold it against you. They might even approve your common sense. But how long does that go on? When would it be safe to go home again, to stay under your own roof, the roof you've worked hard for so you can live under it and shelter your family there? It's all right to send away the small and the weak for a time, but how long can you run yourself? How long can you let a bunch of wet-nosed hoodlums frighten you out of your own home?

I went back to my car and got in and drove toward home, wiping my hands every so often on my trouser legs because they slipped in their own sweat on the wheel. I was still scared.

The house was pitch dark. Naturally. So was the driveway, the garage, the clotted shadows under the trees, under the hedges and the shrubs. I wished I had a spotlight on the car. I wished I had a gun.

I had neither. The bright beams of the headlights swept around as I came up the curving drive, but I could not see anything but the trunk of a tree or a mass of glossy leaves briefly lighted up and then lost again. The garage seemed to be empty too. I shut off the motor and sat listening, holding my stick like a club, but I couldn't hear anything.

I got out and walked to the house.

Not even a breeze rustled in the dark shrubbery. I went inside and locked the door and turned on all the lights, and there was nobody there, and nothing happened.

I leaned against the door, breathing as hard as though I had run all the way out from town. Bush, I thought, whoever you are, I'm going to get you and get you fast, because I can't stand much more of this.

Good night, Bush. Sleep well.

7

KOLESKI called me about eight-thirty the next morning. It seemed like the middle of the day to me, I'd been up so long waiting. I told him what Miller and the other two had told me.

"Bush," he said. "Is that all?"

It didn't sound like much even to me in the cold light of morning. But I said, "It's something, isn't it? It's a name."

"I'll check it out with Juvenile," he said.

"Do you want me to come down there?"

"No, I'll call you. And Sherris, do me a favor? Don't start looking up Bushes in the phone book and battering their doors down."

"I won't," I said, "but it's likely to be a Bush somewhere on this side of town. I made a crasher with that convertible the other day, but the idea was right enough. They were headed this way, coming home."

"I'll keep it in mind. Will you be there if I want you?"

"On the spot."

He hung up. I made another pot of coffee, feeling the absence of Tracey as though some part of myself was missing, thinking how quiet it was without the kids. I did not look up any Bushes in the phone book. I didn't need to. I had already looked them up, made a list of possibles, thrown it away, remade it, and thrown it away again. I didn't do anything. I just twitched and waited.

About eleven the phone rang, and I was almost disappointed when it turned out to be Tracey. Only for a minute, though. I told her what was going on and assured her that I was all right.

"I don't think they're going to pay any attention to that business about the car," I said. "If they'd been going to, they'd have done it last night."

"I hope you're right. Do you think this—this name will lead to anything?"

"Can't tell yet. I'm waiting for a call right now."

"Let me know," she said, kind of small and far away.

"Just as soon as I can."

She hung up, and I asked myself if I was enjoying making her suffer. I could honestly say I was not. Perhaps I was trying to get her to confess before she was caught. I hoped she would.

It was not until after noon that Koleski called again.

"You may just possibly be in luck," he said. "Juvenile has a record on a boy named Bush. Everett Bush, 10710 Shenango Road. That's on your side of town."

"Yes," I said. "One of those slightly crummy new subdivisions, just a mile or so west of here." I tried to keep my voice steady. But Koleski said, "Don't get too hopeful, Sherris. This doesn't have to be the right one. His record doesn't say anything about assault. He's never been accused of anything worse than petty theft and vandalism and he's never been in a corrective institution. Matter of fact, he was very co-operative, readily admitted his guilt, promised not to do it again, and was on a year's probation. There's a coincidence there that kind of interests me, though."

"What's that?"

"His probation ended on April eighteenth."

"The day after they beat me up."

"Yeah," said Koleski. "They just might have been celebrating something more than the big boy's birthday."

He told me to sit tight and hung up. And I waited, and it was hot, and the hours were ten years long.

At quarter after two Koleski's car pulled into the drive. I waited for him at the door. His brows were drawn down into a black line over his eyes, and he looked like one angry Pole. There was a young fellow with him, a man from Juvenile named

Davenport, who had been the Bush boy's probation officer. Koleski made the introduction as though he hated us both, and Davenport grinned.

"Pete's used to the easy stuff," he told me. "Murderers, gunmen, bank robbers, cream puffs like that. He hasn't bucked up against the angry mamas when you come and look hard at their little Junior. The papas only take a sock at you sometimes, but the mamas—wow-*ee*!"

Koleski said, "The boy's parents are bringing him downtown now. I'll call Noddy. We'll see if we can get an identification."

"Maybe I can give you one," I said. "From the voice."

"It had better be a damned positive one from somebody," Koleski said. "Both his parents swear he was at home that night."

"They would, of course," I said, but my heart sank. And Koleski looked straight at me and said evenly, "Before you go down there, Sherris, I want to remind you of your obligations. Don't give me an identification you're not sure of just because you want to pin this on somebody. And remember that you are dealing with a juvenile and not a fugitive from Sing Sing. Can I use your phone?"

"Go ahead."

He called Noddy while I was getting my coat. Then I locked up and we went out together. I said I would take my own car, and for them to go on ahead. After they left I got into my car and sat there for a minute or two, calming down. Koleski was right, of course. I had to be sure. I mustn't try to implicate some kid who might be absolutely innocent.

I tried to call to mind again the voices of the five boys. I had thought I would never forget them as long as I lived. Now I was not so sure. Chuck's I would know, but he had done most of the talking. The short boy's loud, moronic laugh I would know, too. But the others—a grunt, a laugh, a brief few words out of the darkness over my dizzy head, and four months of time now in between. I was not so sure.

I put the automatic-drive lever in reverse and backed out the drive. This was only making things worse. I might as well get downtown and get it over with.

They had the boy in one of the bleak interrogation rooms with the scarred golden-oak chairs and the banged-up tables and the mud-colored linoleum on the floor. His parents were with him. They were a type you can see any Saturday night in any cheap tavern—a thick-necked, red-faced man, ostensibly as jovial as a dancing bear and potentially twice as nasty, and a brassbound blonde with a loud voice. Mr. Bush was not at all jovial right at this moment, and Mrs. Bush was sitting beside her boy, glaring at Koleski and Davenport, and puffing furiously on a cigarette.

The boy himself was sitting quietly, apparently not disturbed by any of it. He looked at me when I came in, and his face was blank and innocent, mildly curious and nothing more.

Mrs. Bush looked at me too. "Are you the one that's accusing my boy? Well, I can tell you, mister, I don't care what you say, Everett was home with his father and me——"

"Please, Mrs. Bush," said Koleski. "Nobody's accused him of anything yet."

"Yeah," said Mr. Bush. "Shut up, Martha. Let 'em handle this their own way. We got nothing to hide." He eyed me as though he was daring me to call him a liar.

Koleski turned to me. "Well?"

"I don't know," I said. "Give me a minute——"

He wasn't a bad-looking boy. Medium height, not fleshed out yet but well-grown and strong. Medium brown hair in a crew cut, a roundish face heavily sunburned, nondescript features, mouth a little slack and sulky perhaps, but nothing you could point to as vicious. Just a boy, like a million other boys that swarm on the campuses of every high school and junior college, good boys, athletes, scholars, the backbone of the future nation. His eyes were blue. They were lifted vaguely toward mine but not quite meeting them. There was nothing in them. They were like pieces of blue glass washed clean by a careful housekeeper.

My heart was pounding and there was a bitter taste in my mouth. I said to Koleski, "Ask him to say something."

Koleski turned to the boy. "What's your name?"

"Everett Bush."

"Where do you live?"

"10710 Shenango Road."

"Where do you go to school?"

"Northside High."

"Do you remember where you were between ten-thirty and eleven on the night of April seventeenth?"

"Yes, sir. I was home."

Koleski looked at me.

It was a very curious feeling. It was as though somebody had opened up the top of my head and poured something scalding hot in through the hole, so that all my veins burned. I took a step toward Everett Bush.

"You weren't at home," I said. "You were on Williams Avenue with four other boys, beating me up."

Everett answered softly, "It wasn't me, mister."

Mrs. Bush stood up. She was a large blonde, very angry, very formidable. She seemed honestly shocked. "You can't accuse my boy of a thing like that," she said.

Everett smiled. "It couldn't have been me. I was home."

"Think carefully, Mr. Sherris," said Koleski, with a note of warning in his voice.

I looked at Mr. Bush and at Mrs. Bush. Two faces against me, hard as adamant.

I looked at Everett. Four months past, four months of brooding. A few brief words out of the night, out of the pain and the fear and the astonishment.

"It sounds like one of them," I said.

"But are you absolutely positive? Could you swear to it in court?"

"I don't suppose," I said, "that I honestly could. Not and make it stick."

Koleski got up from where he had been sitting and nodded to the Bushes. "All right," he said. "You can go now. Thanks for co-operating."

"Co-operating," said Mrs. Bush. "That's what you call it. I call it persecuting a child, that's what I call it. One little black mark, and the child gets blamed for everything that happens."

"Come on," said Mr. Bush, shoving the boy to his feet. "This is a hell of a place to spend my day off."

Everett started toward the door, passing quite close to me.

"Everett," I said, "who's Chuck?"

He stopped, just a little past me, speaking over his shoulder. "Chuck? There's four or five of the guys at school we call Chuck. Which one do you mean?"

"You know which one I mean. The big one. And the one you call 'goof.' And Bill."

He shook his head. "I don't know who you're talking about, mister—did you say your name was Sherris?"

Koleski said quickly, before I could answer, "Ever heard that name before?"

"Yes, sir," said Everett.

"Where?"

"In the paper. About how he chased that car, only it was the wrong one."

Koleski sighed. "Okay," he said. "That's all."

Mr. Bush stopped in front of me, looking me up and down. "So that was you," he said. He turned to Koleski. "Seems to me like you ought to lock this bird up instead of letting him make trouble for any kid he happens to pick on."

Everett turned in the doorway. "Honest, mister," he said. "It wasn't me."

And now for the first time he looked directly at me for a flicker of a second, and for the first time there was something in his eyes, something dark and secret and triumphant, and laughing.

Then they were gone away down the corridor, out of my grasp.

"Noddy couldn't identify him either," said Koleski. "Not positively. He said if it was the boy, he's had his hair cut short since then and he looks different. I'm sorry, Sherris."

"I think he was one of them, just the same," I said. I was still looking after him out the door, remembering that look in his eyes, remembering the quiver of my own flesh as he passed close to me. "I know he is."

"You weren't so sure of that just now."

"You asked me if I could swear to it in court. Suppose I did. Suppose I stood in front of a magistrate and swore that his voice sounded like one of the boy's, and that he looked at me in a certain way, and I got a certain feeling in my bones. How much of a hearing could you get on that?"

"He's got a good cast-iron alibi, Sherris."

I turned to Davenport. "You know these people. Would they lie about that?"

He shrugged. "It's a natural reaction. I couldn't say they would. I'd say they might, if the penalty looked worse than the offence."

"How do you mean?"

"Well, suppose the boy came home late and said he'd got into a little fuss around a saloon. No harm done, just a little fuss, see? But he's still on probation. Minors are forbidden by law to enter such places and demand to be served and that goes double for him. At the very least, there'd be trouble about it, an extension of probation, investigation of home conditions, red tape. It's easier for everybody if the parents just say he didn't go out at all that night. He wouldn't have to mention anything else."

"You know what you've done, Davenport?" said Koleski wearily. "You've just pulled the pin and handed the grenade to Sherris."

"Don't worry," I said. "I'm just trying to think." I sat down. I didn't feel good. Reaction, disappointment, an absolutely vicious hate boiling up in me without my asking for it, frustration—I was glad Everett and his parents were gone, or I might have made more trouble for Koleski in spite of myself. "Couldn't you have him watched? If I'm right, and he is one of the bunch, he'd lead us to Chuck and the rest, and then we'd have them."

Koleski lighted another cigarette and sat on the edge of the table, studying me.

"What is it?" I asked him.

"I wish I knew," he said. "I wish I knew how much is being honestly sure, and how much is wanting something so bad that the whole world has got warped around it."

"I wish I could tell you," I said.

"Wait here," he said. "I'll see what I can do."

I waited. Davenport said he would check out Northside High for a possible lead, but he was not hopeful because of the lack of any identification, and because Everett himself had not seemed at all worried. Davenport figured the boys probably went to different schools and did their running around together off the campus. Everett's parents apparently did not know or care much about who he went with, and Davenport said that was one big thing that was wrong with people these days. He wished me luck and went away.

It was hot and stifling in the room and the air was stale. I sat looking at the chair where Everett Bush had sat, and all of a sudden I thought with the sharpest and most curious surprise how strange it was that I had got into such a mess, and why I was sitting here in this dingy room in Police Headquarters, looking death and damnation at an empty chair.

Koleski came back shaking his head. "No dice. There isn't a team of men to spare. I told you we're having a busy season." He paused and then he said, "That's most of the truth, Sherris. The rest of it is that we could dig up a team if the skipper felt there was a real reason for it. Under the circumstances, he doesn't."

After a while he said again, "I'm sorry."

"Listen," I said. "Could I hire a detective? A private detective. Is there any law against that?"

"Not that I know of," said Koleski. "You could try it, anyhow." He wrote two names and addresses on a scrap of memo paper and handed it to me. "Both these guys are all right. Don't say I sent you."

"Okay," I said. "Thanks." We shook hands. "Can I buy you a drink?"

"Some time," he said. "When I'm off duty."

"It's a deal."

I started out.

"Uh—Sherris——"

"Yes?"

"Where'd they teach you to be so stubborn?"

"The Army," I said, "told us never to give in to aggressors."

"Hm," he said. "I was in the Marines myself. Active service?"

"Occupation stuff. They got me between wars."

"Well," said Koleski, "don't push it too far, that's all. Let me know."

I said I would. I went out into the street, baking under the August sun, and headed for the first of the two addresses on Koleski's slip of paper.

8

THE first man was already tied up and couldn't do anything for me for at least a couple of weeks. The second one, a Thomas Finelli, was in court giving evidence in a divorce case, but his secretary, a very young girl who said Finelli was her uncle, seemed to think he would be glad to talk to me.

I asked when.

She frowned, turning over the pages of an appointment book.

"He'll be in court probably till five and then he has to go straight to Newbridge for the party. It's their golden wedding— my grandparents', that is. So it'll have to be tomorrow, say around nine-thirty? Unless for some reason he has to go back to court. Maybe you better call before you come all the way in."

"Will he stop by here after he's through in court?"

"Oh yes. He has to pick me up."

"Maybe he can give me a minute then. It won't take long. I'll be back."

She was unhappy about that, but I didn't give her any chance to talk me out of it. I wanted to know. If Finelli couldn't or wouldn't take me on, I would have to find somebody else and I didn't want to waste any more time than I had to.

I killed an hour or so around town, using part of it to buy Tracey a present, a bottle of a particular perfume I knew she liked but usually wouldn't buy because it was too expensive. I owed her that much anyway. She had taken good care of me these past months. Better, sometimes, than I deserved. She might have been inspired by a guilty conscience but that was beside the point. I had the perfume sent.

At four-thirty I went back to Finelli's small office on the fifth floor of a building no dingier than most of the old unlovely structures in the Mall's Ford business district, where hardly anything has been built new since the turn of the century, and where between the mill smoke and the winter soot from thousands of chimneys it doesn't much matter anyway, given a couple of years. He had not come in yet. His niece was all combed and lipsticked and ready to go, with the desk cleaned off slick as a whistle. I sat down and began to work my way through a stack of movie magazines and true confessions. The girl took one sulkily out of her desk drawer, where she'd been hoarding it, and we read together until Finelli came in.

He was a square stocky man, somewhere in his middle forties, and he had a competent look about him. He did not seem very happy to see me but he listened politely while I explained that what I wanted wouldn't take long.

"Real important?"

I said it was to me.

"Okay. Come on inside."

I followed him into the inner office and he shut the door. The room was about ten feet square, with a desk, two chairs, and some filing cabinets. He motioned me to sit down.

"Now, then," he said, "what's your trouble?"

I told him, and it surprised even me how few words it took when you boiled it right down to the essentials. He listened, asking an occasional question, taking notes.

"You want me to shadow the boy, find out who his associates are, and whether they fit these descriptions."

"That's it."

"Of course, the boy might play it smart. He might figure he'd be tailed and stay away from the rest of the gang for a while."

"He might, yes, although he seemed pretty sure of himself. But if he doesn't see you——"

"He won't."

"Well, sooner or later, if I'm right about these other beatings, he'll go back to the others. I'm willing to wait."

"How long, Mr. Sherris? I'm not exorbitantly expensive, but I do cost."

"Any reasonable length of time. As of right now I am not worrying about the money."

Finelli nodded. "Just don't expect results by tomorrow morning, that's all. And of course you know the boy may very well be innocent."

"That's why I want to hire you, to find out."

"Are these names and addresses correct?"

I said they were, and also my telephone number.

"All right, Mr. Sherris. I'll let you know as soon I have anything to report."

"Thanks," I said. "That's a load off my mind. Have a good time." He looked surprised, and I added, "At the golden wedding."

He laughed. "Too much spaghetti and *vino*. I'll feel like hell in the morning."

We all went out of the office together, and I told him I would send him a check for the retainer in the morning. Then I was out in the street again, at a hot five-thirty, wondering what to do.

What I wanted to do was drive up to the lake and spend the night there. But when I thought it over I decided not to. If the Bush boy was one of the gang that had beaten me, the fact that I had managed to track him down and get him hauled in for questioning might have some repercussions.

It would be hitting much closer to home than that foolish business of chasing the wrong car—about which Everett Bush had been very fully informed for a kid who had no personal interest in it. He knew I was still suspicious of him and, even though he had managed to talk his way out of it this time with the help of his parents, he might feel that something ought to be done to discourage me from going any further.

The boys might make some overt move, something that would give them away, or at least make it possible for me to bring the police in on it again. One definite piece of evidence against any one of them was all I needed.

This sounded rather dangerous, but I had no intention of exposing myself to any danger. And I couldn't see that I would be running any more risk than I was liable to run any night now.

No risk at all, if Everett was as innocent as he said he was.

I hoped the day would come when I could say for sure that somebody was definitely innocent or guilty of something.

I went home.

On the way I picked up some cans and a steak. It was still full daylight when I got to the house, with several hours more of it to go. The neighbors were out of doors in the shady places, trying to cool off, and there were children playing and cars going up and down the street. There was no sign that anyone but the mailman had been around.

I went inside and bolted the door and looked carefully through every room, making sure the windows were locked as I went. There was no one there. There was no one in the cellar, either. I got a good heavy wrench from the toolbox and took it upstairs and laid it where it would be handy, just in case. Then I called Tracey.

"You don't know how I wish you'd give this up," she said, when I had told her about Everett Bush and Finelli.

I thought I did but I only told her not to worry, that I was taking very good care of myself. Pudge had been put to bed but Bets talked to me a minute, all about the lake and how she was learning to swim. After I hung up the house seemed awfully still and lonesome.

While the steak was broiling I sat in the kitchen and drank a beer and listened to the quiet. The world was bright and normal outside the windows, and here I sat, in the stale, stifling silence, a prisoner in my own house.

First I was furious and then I felt like a fool. Probably nothing would happen anyway. Probably I was dreaming things up out of whole cloth, basing conclusions on fears and guesses and wishful thinking. I opened the side door again and took my dinner out on the terrace and ate it there.

It wasn't a bad dinner, but it reminded me at every bite that Tracey hadn't cooked it. When I had finished it and washed up there was nothing to do but wait.

I went back out on the terrace and smoked and watched the shadows lengthening across the lawn. When it was dusk I would move into the house and sit with the lights out and watch.

A hell of a way to spend an evening.

I was just getting up to go inside, somewhere between seven-thirty and eight o'clock, when the phone rang.

I thought it might be Tracey calling back and I jumped for it, not stopping to lock the door behind me. But when I had my hand on it I suddenly thought that it might be one of the boys checking to see if I was there. My heart began to pound, and I let the phone ring three times before I answered. I was ashamed of myself but I couldn't help it. And I found out right there that I did not, under any circumstances or for any reason, want them coming around to see me.

It was not Tracey on the phone, and it was not one of those silences, pregnant with menace and ending with a click as soon as you have said hello. It was George Warren, head of the Credit Department at Valley Steel. The voice of God. In short, my boss. And it was queer how far George Warren and Valley Steel had slipped away from me in these past weeks. From filling most of my waking hours they had dwindled to a memory of something interesting and important, but long ago superseded, like a game you used to play as a child. I suppose it's like that when you start taking dope. The dream and the sensation crowd out reality. Five boys and a broken leg had done that for me.

"Are you busy tonight, Walt?"

"No," I said. "I'm not doing anything."

"I was thinking I might run over and see you, if you're feeling up to it."

The reality began to make itself felt again.

"Of course," I said. "Matter of fact, George, I was just going to call you and——"

"Fine, fine," he said. "Around eight-thirty?"

"Great," I said, and he hung up.

No matter who hits you over the head or how mad you get about it, the living still has to be made, the wife and kiddies fed.

I got another beer and sat on the terrace drinking it, close by the door and ready to jump as the light got dimmer and the shadows began to shape up under the trees. I was thinking about Valley Steel and accounts, and regretting to my soul that I had got rid of the Luger I brought back from Germany, as a concession to Tracey's nerves and the prying fingers of my eldest.

69

I had the yard lights on, and from where I sat I could see the driveway. There was a light at the garage, one at the front of the house, and one here on the terrace. This last one I did not have on, for obvious reasons. The others gave broad circles of illumination, but there was quite a lot of yard, and plenty of dusk and darkness in between. I thought that if this went on much longer I would have lights installed to cover the whole grounds.

Then Warren's car turned into the drive, and I thought of my job and the inadvisability of letting George get any idea that my mental balance was in any way upset. The business of the convertible was going to be enough to explain away. As I went to the front door to let him in I shoved the wrench down out of sight behind a chair.

George was a pretty nice fellow as bosses go. If I lived long enough and kept my head on straight, I would one day fill his fancy swivel chair in the inner office. He was beginning to develop a fine executive-type bulge in front, and a smaller one running laterally between the ears. These back-of-the-neck bulges seem to be in the nature of service stripes, adding one at each promotion so that the boys at the very top may have several of them. George was on his way.

He stayed with me for an hour and a half, sitting on the terrace because it was far too hot inside, drinking a couple of modest drinks. He asked all about my health and how the case was progressing and how the family was, and then he switched to general topics of office gossip and shoptalk. He was as friendly as anyone could be and never once did he come baldly out and say it in so many words, but the implication was absolutely plain. If I wanted my job I had better quit fooling around and get back to it.

I didn't blame him. As long as I was legitimately laid up it was one thing, but they couldn't carry me forever while I played detective and chased shadows.

"Take it easy at first," said George. "If you find yourself getting tired, go home. We'll try not to load you down too much."

"I'm feeling pretty good," I said. "A little slow getting around, but that's all."

"Fine," said George. "Now of course it's up to you, Walt——"

"This is Thursday," I said. "Fag end of the week. How about Monday morning?"

"Great," said George. "Splendid. Believe me, Walt, we'll all be glad to have you back."

I said I would be glad to be back and I meant it. It was right, it was normal, it was the world I used to live in. It would be good to get out of this atmosphere of violence and skulking fear. You could get mired too deep in it. You could get lost in it. Let Finelli worry about the case now. That's reality to him, that's what he's paid for. Get back to your own, for a while at least, until something comes up that will end the whole ugly business for good.

I was glad George had come. I had needed a breath of dull conventional sanity to blow the cobwebs out of my brain. I walked him back to his car, the short way, across the lawn from the terrace to the drive. It had clouded over, and there was a flicker of lightning in the south. George said it looked like rain, and I said we could use some to cool things off. He drove away, and I walked back toward the terrace.

It was only a little way, twenty-five or thirty feet.

I didn't make it.

9

THERE were only three of them this time. The tall skinny boy, the elusive Bill who knew me but whom I could not find, and the boy who might have been Everett Bush were not there.

But Chuck was.

He got me around the neck from behind, and when I tried to turn and hit him the others caught my arms. They wrestled me in under the boughs of a maple tree, where the shadows were thick and heavy to hide them, and they held me there. I had heard them, perhaps a fraction of a second before they grabbed me, but not soon enough to do anything about it. They must have left their car out of sight down the street and come creeping in among the shrubs at a time when both George and I were in the house, avoiding the lights and then lying patiently in wait until my guest should go and give them a chance at me.

Chuck said, "Stand still."

The bend of his elbow was just under my chin, forcing my head back into his chest, shutting off my wind. The short stocky boy with the loud laugh had hold of my right arm. He was twisting it more than he needed to. The other boy had my left. I had dropped my stick. I stood still, in a sheer cold panic of fright. I hadn't started yet to get mad.

"That's good," said Chuck. He let up a bit so I could breathe. There was something almost caressing, almost friendly about his voice, as though we were old buddies and understood each other. "Not so hard there, goof, you don't want to break his arm, do you?" The goof laughed, and Chuck said rather sharply, "Not now, remember? We just came to talk to Mr. Sherris."

I could feel his breath on the back of my neck. I hated him. I wanted to kill him. I wanted to get him down on the ground and stomp him and tear him into pieces and throw the pieces away.

I said, "You want to talk to me about Everett."

"Everett?" said Chuck. "Who's that?"

"Everett Bush," I said. "The boy who isn't here tonight. Or one of them. He'd be afraid to come, naturally, but where's Bill? Did he wash out on you?"

"Mr. Sherris," said Chuck, in that oddly caressing tone. "I came here to do you a favor. Don't make it hard for me."

He tightened the vise around my neck. Stars swam in front of my eyes and my ears boomed.

"I don't know any Everett Bush," said Chuck. "And Bill's none of your business. Now will you listen?"

He relaxed his arm again, and I said I would.

With his free hand he took a piece of paper out of his pocket and held it in my face. I couldn't see what it was, but he told me. It was the piece about how I had chased that convertible.

"You're lucky," said Chuck, "that it was the wrong one. And you better not do that any more, Mr. Sherris. You know what would happen to you if you caught the right one?"

He dropped the paper suddenly and hit me on the side of the head, just hard enough to make it ring.

"I know you, Mr. Sherris," he said. "I've got an interest in you, a kind of special interest. You were a mistake. I don't often make mistakes and I don't like to be reminded of them. Don't remind me any more."

"Oh, that's fine," I said, "but it isn't so easy. You gave me something to make me think of you every time I move, and more than that you——"

You threatened my family, I was going to say. You wrote my wife a letter. I couldn't say it. I couldn't give Tracey the lie out of the mouth of this wretched pervert. I couldn't even mention her to him. She would tell me about it herself or nobody would.

It was very strange. I had lived this minute over several thousand times, only in my visualization I was the victor and the boys were safely in custody. Now, with this one difference, the

73

moment was here and all I had to do was ask Chuck, Did you write my wife a threatening letter. And I couldn't.

"More than that I what?" he asked politely.

"I was going to say," I said, "you made me mad."

They had a good laugh over that. "Hey, Chuck, you hear that?" cried the goof. "We made him mad." He hit me in the pit of the belly. "I'll bet that makes you even madder, doesn't it, mister?"

"Shut up," said Chuck. "Don't distract him. I want him to get this clear through his head. Mr. Sherris?"

"Yeah."

"You understand. I'm warning you. Leave us alone."

"What'll you do, kill me?" A slow heat was coming up from where the stocky boy had hit me. It spread all over me, burning out the fear. You get to a certain stage. After that you're not responsible.

"I might," said Chuck, very softly. "We haven't tried that yet. We might like it."

"What do you think gives you the right?" I asked him.

"I feel like it."

"You feel like it. Who do you think you are—God?"

"As far as you're concerned, Sherris," he said, "I am."

And he snapped my head back, just to show me.

I jerked my arms in with all my strength, and at the same time I kicked back as hard as I could with my bad leg, weighted with the heavy steel brace. It hit Chuck solidly above the ankle. He roared with the unexpected pain, and his arm loosened around my neck. I threw myself forward, yelling at the top of my lungs for help. It was a quiet suburban neighborhood, but it was not deserted like Williams Avenue. I saw my stick lying on the grass just beyond the shadow of the tree and I went for it. Somebody, I don't know which one it was or whether it was more than one of them, knocked me down flat. I was groggy, but I heard a voice calling my name and I answered it. "Here!" I shouted. "Here, Joe, quick!"

A light came on in Joe Thompson's yard next door. I got my hand on my stick and rolled over and began to lash out with it at the poised and startled shapes of the boys. I could see the paler blurs that were their faces, but they were just blurs, without features. Chuck was calling me a foul name, over and over in a flat vicious monotone. He was out of reach, but I hit the stocky boy a good solid belt. He cried out and jumped back, and I made a whistling cut at the third one, but he had already started to run away.

Joe Thompson had now come around the end of the fence that divided our properties and was in my yard, calling to know what was the matter.

The stocky boy muttered about getting out of there. He started to run too. Chuck had stopped his cursing now, but I could hear him panting in the dark and feel him looking at me. "Come on, yellowbelly," I said. "Come on, where I can get at you." I was not thinking very straight. I just wanted to kill him.

He didn't answer. He breathed, like an animal. Lights were springing on in White's yard, my neighbor on the other side. I was trying to get up.

"I'll get you," I said. "If it's the last thing I do."

I could see his head turn quickly, looking toward Joe Thompson, looking toward White's.

"If you ever come here again I'll kill you," I said.

He turned and run.

"I'll kill you," I shouted after him. "I'll kill you. I'll——"

Joe Thompson put his hand on my shoulder. "They're gone now. Are you all right? Sit tight till I make sure."

He went after them, not as though he had any real desire to catch up. I could hear somebody, probably Chuck, thrashing his way through the line of shrubs that hedged the street. A minute later I heard a car start up, around the curve. It roared away. Then I heard Joe Thompson talking to Andy White, and presently they both came back to where I was.

I was standing up now. I told them I wasn't hurt, which was true, but my leg was killing me. It was still tender for all this banging around. They helped me back to the house and Andy poured me a good stiff drink. He was a lawyer, and Joe Thompson was sales manager for a steel firm. They were both good friends of mine in a casual sort of way. They looked excited and upset, and Joe kept asking if he should call the police first or a doctor.

"The police," I said. I kept thinking how good it had felt to lay my stick across the stocky boy's legs. I hoped I had really hurt him, but from the way he ran I doubted it. "You didn't get a look at them, did you?"

They both shook their heads. "Not more than just a glimpse of them running away," said Joe. He picked up the phone.

I sat there, trying to remember what I had said to Chuck, not being very sure about that except that it hadn't been exactly wise to threaten him, but remembering very clearly the way he had looked at me there in the dark, the way he had felt, like a hungry thing prowling beyond the light.

"Wrong," I said. "All wrong."

"What is?" asked Andy.

"That boy. Chuck. Wrong, something left out of him."

"Crazy?" said Andy.

"No, not that. Different." I was hunting for a word and couldn't find it. I looked at Joe talking into the telephone. "Communication. No communication. We could talk for a hundred years and neither one of us would ever know what the other one was thinking, or why."

"It doesn't excuse him," said Andy. "Legally or morally."

"I'm not even sure it explains it," I said. "But when he had his arm around my neck there, my life literally under his hand, where he could feel it, where he could stop it in a minute if he wanted to, he was—at ease. As though he'd finally made contact. Maybe that's the only way he can make contact with the people around him, through domination. Through violence."

"Must be damned hard on his friends," said Andy.

Joe Thompson put the phone down. "They'll be right out," he said, and started for the door. "Back in a minute, Walt. I want to tell my wife."

"Tell mine too," said Andy. He sat down beside me. "What about the others?"

"I'll hazard a guess. One familiar type of sadistic moron. One kid brought up in an atmosphere of brutality, dishing out a little, of what he's always had to take. One—well, compensating for

76

something or other, I suppose, or just exercising a naturally dirty nature. And one that doesn't seem to belong with the others in the first place. But Chuck is the catalyst. He gives them all direction and meaning."

Andy looked at me sharply. "Aren't you dreaming this up a little, Walt? They seem to me to be like any ordinary bunch of young hoodlums, of which we have far too many these days."

"Yes," I said. "But how ordinary is ordinary? I mean, you can just as easily say an ordinary Dillinger type, or an ordinary Marquis de Sade. They weren't either one of them unique. They just happened to get famous."

He decided not to argue it with me. Joe came back after a bit, and then the police came, two officers I didn't know in a prowl car. They asked all the pertinent questions and went over the grounds with a flashlight, retrieving the piece of torn newspaper that Chuck had dropped and placing it carefully in an envelope. Then one of them went off up the street to ask if any of the neighbors had seen the car.

It had apparently been parked well away from any house, on a stretch where nothing had yet been built. Two or three people remembered having noticed a light-colored convertible, probably gray, but not the license number nor who got out of it.

I told the officers I would be down in the morning to talk to Koleski. They said they would keep an eye on the neighborhood in case the boys came back, and advised me to keep my door locked. They left. I considered calling Tracey but decided against it. Let her have her night's sleep. Morning would be time enough.

Both Andy and Joe tried to talk me into spending the rest of the night at their place. After all, they said, why be a hero? And I couldn't see much reason myself at this moment. I didn't believe the boys would come back, but I knew I was going to leap and twitch at every sound no matter what my common sense told me. I picked Joe's place because the guest room was on the ground floor and I didn't feel like climbing stairs.

Joe brought my pajamas and a bottle to put beside the bed, and his wife made me welcome, and that was fine. But after I crawled in between the sheets I couldn't sleep. I felt safe enough but I kept going over what had happened and how my plans had got messed up and everything had gone wrong. I cursed George Warren and wondered what would come next, who would make the move and what it would be. I turned and twisted and raged and sweated, in a waking nightmare of frustration.

I pulled on the bottle until I couldn't feel my leg ache any more, and the frustration and the anger dimmed, and just before I finally dropped off one simple idea came clear and shone in my mind with an ominous light.

Tomorrow, I thought, I will get myself a gun.

That may be an answer, I thought, one answer anyway, to Chuck and Everett and those faceless others. But to Tracey there is no answer. And now there won't be one unless she gives it to me.

Anyway, I thought, I'm glad I didn't ask.

10

I was still glad of it in the morning, when I called Tracey. It wasn't much use trying to keep her from knowing what had happened. There would almost certainly be a mention of it in the paper, on a news broadcast, or in the mouth of a helpful friend, and then she would be frantic. Better to tell her myself.

I did, as matter-of-factly as I could, stressing the idea that I was perfectly all right. I heard her sharp shocked sigh on the other end of the line, and then she said, "I told you, Walt. I told you."

"Yes, you did."

"Surely you'll stop now."

"I don't think that's possible, even if I wanted to."

"Of course it's possible. What do you mean, it isn't possible?"

"Well, in the first place, I lost my temper and told them to go to hell. In the second place, I can't stop the police. And anyway, how could I convince them that I had quit? They're irresponsible, Tracey. They're dangerous. I can't just cover my head and pretend they're not there, not with that kind of a threat hanging over me." I added, "Over us."

"Over us," she repeated slowly, and then a silence came to me from her end of the wire and spread all through the empty house around me so I could hear the faint ticking of the walls as the sun began to heat them up.

It went on so long that the operator asked if we had completed our call.

"No," said Tracey. "No, wait. Walt, did they tell you——"

Again silence, and I thought I could hear her heart beating, but I suppose it was only the pulsation of the line.

"—about the letter," she finished.

"Why, no," I said.

"Didn't you ask them? I thought——"

"What did you think?"

"I don't know. I don't know, Walt. I feel so queer these days, not as though I was living in the real world at all."

"I know what you mean."

"I'm frightened. All the time, every minute." Her voice went up into the borderline register of hysteria. "Why won't you stop it and go away where you'll be safe and not frighten me to death?"

"Honey," I said. "Leave my job, and our house, our families?"

"I have to see you," she said, and now her voice had slid back down to a flat half whisper.

"No. You stay right where you are till this is over. If I have a gun I can take care of myself but I can't take you on too."

"Walt, I have to see you."

"I'm not going to argue with you. You stay there. I'll come up as soon as I can. I have to go downtown now, Koleski's waiting for me. I'll call you."

I hung up and went out of the house quickly so I could not hear the phone if she called back. The garden looked beautiful. There had been some rain late in the night. The earth in the beds was moist and dark, the flowers were bright, and all the green things were clean-washed and shining. If I have a gun I can take care of myself. It sounded silly.

Then I looked at the maple tree and the scuffed places under it in the grass.

I drove downtown to Headquarters. And all the way, without consciously thinking about it, I was expecting a gray convertible to come at me from out of some sudden crossroad, driven by a tall strong handsome boy. I wondered who his parents were. I wondered if they knew, or suspected, what their child was. Whoever they were, I felt sorry for them.

Koleski already had the report but he had me give him the story anyway, questioning me pretty closely, especially about the threats and my reference to Everett Bush.

"Chuck denied knowing Everett Bush," he said.

"Naturally. He was lying."

"You state that very positively."

"I am positive. It's obvious. Everett told them he'd been traced and questioned. He told them they'd better get me off his neck. So they came."

Koleski smoothed the crumpled clipping on his desk, the same one Chuck had brought and dropped.

"This seems clear enough."

"Of course they'd lay it onto that," I said impatiently. "They wouldn't be likely to lay it on Everett, would they?"

"No," said Koleski, and sighed. "Unfortunately, I can't either."

"Chuck's a smart boy," I said. "He's only made one mistake so far. He said so."

"What's that?"

"Me. But he's made another, only he doesn't know it yet." Koleski waited, and I told him, "He thinks he's going to get away with it. Look, I want a permit."

"For a gun?" said Koleski, looking at me.

"For what else?"

He continued to look at me. "I like you, Sherris. I'd hate to have to bring you in here on a bad rap."

"I'm not going hunting," I said. "My life has been threatened. I know I'm a grown man and therefore not sacred like a child, but it seems as though I ought to have the right to protect myself."

Koleski sighed again. He picked up the phone and talked for a minute and then put it down again. "They'll fix you up," he said. "Just be careful, will you? I mean that."

He laid the clipping back in the report folder, and I knew what he was thinking.

"No," I said. "Nothing like that. I'm leaving this strictly to Finelli. I'm going back to work Monday."

He grunted as though he would like to believe me but couldn't, quite. I left him. Before I was halfway down the hall he passed me, with two other men, all going somewhere in a hurry. As he had said before, he was a busy man, and what's a beating in this world of homicides and holdups, arsons and kidnapings?

I went down the street and bought a .38 automatic.

Finelli was waiting for me, in answer to a phone call I had made. He listened while I told my story again, asking much the same questions that Koleski had. I don't know how much of my insistence that last night's visit was directly connected with Everett Bush seemed convincing to him, but he said he would go ahead with the case, keeping it in mind.

"If he did contact the other boys yesterday," he said, "it was probably by phone, and the chances are that he'll stay away from them for some time. Not only in case he's being watched, but to keep his parents from learning the truth. They might have different ideas about covering for him if they did."

"Take all the time you need," I said, "but I don't think you'll have too long to wait." I was thinking of the way those other beatings were spaced out.

"Okay," he said. "It's your money."

"Also my neck," I told him. I gave him my office phone to use after the first of the week if he needed it. Then I decided to go round to where my brother-in-law makes his living selling insurance and see if I could have lunch with him. I was getting lonesome.

Vince was glad to see me, and sure, we could have lunch together. But he had somebody with him. Would I wait? I said I would and sat down in the outer office. His girl, Peggy, hadn't seen me since before I got hurt, and she was flatteringly anxious to talk about it between taking calls and making appointments. I had been there perhaps fifteen minutes when Peggy, answering the phone and explaining that Mr. Farrel was busy, suddenly looked at me and said,

"Well now, that's an odd thing. Mrs. Farrel—your brother's right here. Do you want to talk to him?"

I got up, startled, and took the phone. "Mae?" I said. "Were you trying to get me? What's wrong?"

Mae's voice sounded agitated, a little impatient, a little angry. "It's Tracey," she said. "She just left here."

"What do you mean, she just left there? She's at the lake——"

"Oh no, she's not. Her father drove her down. He wouldn't leave her at your place when he found you weren't there, so they

82

came here—and the minute his back was turned she called a cab and took off."

"Took off where?"

"Home. Your home. She says she belongs there and that's where she's going to stay, no matter what. I don't like the way she's acting, Walt, and furthermore, she told me all about last night, and if you want my opinion, Walt, *you're* acting like a damn fool——"

I didn't want her opinion, not at that moment. I handed the phone back to Peggy and went out. I wanted to run to my car, and it was an awful feeling not to be able to. It seemed to me that the block between Vince's office and the lot where I was parked had stretched out since the last time I had seen it until it was two miles long.

The way home seemed even longer. I was an old man before I made it. I thought, I wasn't cut out for a life like this, my nerves aren't good, they aren't standing up well. I'm afraid all the time now, of everything and nothing, for myself and everyone around me.

They say in action you get conditioned to fear. I was never in action, so I don't know. But at least there you would know who the enemy was and where he was and how he could be expected to strike.

I thought, I am becoming a shivering coward. It's a bright hot summer day, my wife has come down from the lake to see me, and she is waiting in our house. What's wrong with that?

The wrongness is because of five shadows in the dark, three shadows underneath the maple tree.

The wrongness is because of violence, senseless and reasonless and beyond prediction because it has no cause.

Yet it must have a cause. Not in me, not in any of the people that it wounds and hurts, but in the deep unknown of the secret individual, the hungry, doubtful, fearful, predatory *I* crouched in eternal isolation behind its ramparts of flesh and bone, peering at the world.

Money makes a Dillinger, but what makes a De Sade? Why will one child, too young for social hypocrisy, weep with pity for a dead kitten, while another, in solemn and intense excitement,

83

bloodily destroys every small defenseless creature that comes its way? Who can say for sure what dark images of need and pleasure these strange children pursue?

Sunlight poured brilliantly through the green overhang of the trees. It made the road shimmer. I was beginning to hate that road. Too much had happened on it, at its end and its beginning.

I reached the house. There was no one in sight. I left my car in the drive and went as fast as I could up to the front door. It was open behind the aluminum storm door that had its screen insert in place for the summer. I pulled this open too and went in, calling Tracey's name.

There was no answer.

11

For a minute I was terrified and then I saw her, sitting quite quietly on the couch, her back very straight, her head bowed a little to one side, her hands folded in her lap. She looked almost as though she was posing for an effect, and yet I knew she wasn't. She wasn't conscious of herself at all. She looked up at me when I came into the room, and there was a stark honesty in her face that was pitiful to see. She was not hiding any more, from herself or me.

"Walt," she said, "there wasn't any letter."

Just like that.

But it wasn't enough. She had to go on.

"I was afraid. That was a terrible night when they called me and said you'd been hurt and I went down to the hospital. I saw you lying there in the bed, and you weren't Walt any more, you were far away from me, gone." She made a pushing gesture in the air. Her eyes had not wavered from mine. "They said you might always be like that, they couldn't tell yet. Not you at all, just— something in a bed. I ran away, Walt. I did. I made it up about the threatening letter so it wouldn't seem as though I had, but I did. And afterward I was ashamed. I was ashamed to come back."

Now she had said it, and there was no more. She sat still, watching me, a patient figure, asking for nothing, not pity or forgiveness or even understanding.

"Tracey," I said. "Dear——"

I sat down beside her and put my arms around her. Her mouth trembled, but her body was passive and withdrawn.

"I ran away," she said, "when you needed me the most."

"You came back," I said.

"You knew, didn't you? All along."

I pulled her closer. "It's all over now."

"You knew, but you never said anything and you didn't even ask the boys——"

Now she made me feel ashamed.

"Tracey," I said. "You're my wife, aren't you? From now on?"

"Could you ever trust me again?"

"I'd better," I said. "You're the only wife I've got."

She said a word or two more, but I couldn't understand them. The trembling was all over her now. She began to cry and then she had her arms around me under my jacket and was pressing her head against my chest, tight, very tight, as though she wanted to get right inside me, to show by the merging of her body with mine that we were indeed, as it says in the ceremony, one flesh. Or perhaps it was only that very human, very animal need for comfort, the need to be held and reassured. Whichever it was, I didn't care. I held her as long as she wanted, until she had stopped crying and stopped trembling and was just Tracey, my wife, warm and quiet in my arms, the way she always had been.

No, not that way. Not quite that way ever again. That was the young us, before we had ever had to think about courage and forgiving and our own shortcomings. We were different people now. Sometimes it doesn't take years to grow older. Sometimes it can be done in a few weeks, a few days, a few minutes. We had aged. We looked at each other, and we knew it, but neither of us said anything. We kissed, and that was different too, not less loving but more gentle. We knew, and understood.

I got up and opened all the doors and windows wide to let the sunlight in. I guess it was one of those broadly symbolic gestures, but I wasn't thinking about it. I was thinking that I hadn't realized until now how forlorn and deserted I had felt, and how much of my fear came from that subconscious sense of being alone.

Tracey came behind me as I opened the door onto the terrace. She was crying again, but smiling too. She said, "I'll go get us some lunch."

86

That was the beginning of a good period. It lasted for nine days, until the Saturday night when Finelli was killed. After that things seemed to go in a blind downhill rush, but those nine days were fine. Part of them I spent at the lake with Tracey's folks and the children. Most of them I spent at my desk in the offices of Valley Steel, putting on the familiar routine again piece by piece, like an old comfortable suit of clothes. All of them I spent with Tracey. For that short time we were back in the real world again, doing real things, and the only voice from the shadowland was Finelli's, calling occasionally to say that he had nothing to report. The boys did not show themselves again. Perhaps Chuck thought that in spite of what I said I had taken his warning seriously. Certainly nothing happened in that time to make him think otherwise.

Then early on Sunday morning the phone rang. Tracey climbed sleepily out of bed to answer it. She came back almost at once, no longer sleepy, and said, "It's for you, Walt. It's that detective. Koleski."

I hobbled to the phone. "Yes?" I said. "What's up?"

Koleski's voice sounded distant and impersonal. "When was the last time you heard from Finelli?"

"Yesterday morning. Why?"

"What did he tell you?"

"Nothing. He didn't have anything to tell."

"But he was still working for you?"

"Yes. What's happened?"

"He was still trailing the Bush boy?"

"That's what I was paying him for."

"Do you know whether he was following the boy last night?"

"I suppose he was."

"But do you know for sure?"

"Well," I said, "no, I don't suppose I could swear he was. For God's sake, Koleski. What is this?"

"Finelli ran his car off the road last night about midnight. He's dead. Killed instantly."

That hit me, as it does when it happens to someone you know. I thought of the niece and the golden-wedding party.

"How did it happen?" I asked. "And where?"

"The curve on Route 422, just this side of the strip mine. He was headed west. There were no witnesses. There was *apparently* no other car involved." He stressed that one word lightly. "Someone had burned rubber on the road there, close by, but there's no definite connection."

"I wonder," I said. Suddenly I was flushed and hot, and my temples were pounding. "Listen," I said. "Listen, he was shadowing Everett Bush. Everett has laid low for days now but last night he must have thought he was safe and joined the others. Finelli followed them. He must have seen them do something, and then somehow they spotted him. They drive fast, those kids. They drive like hell. I'll bet they ran him off the road."

"I figured that was about what you would figure," said Koleski. "But I was hoping you might have something definite to back it up." I could almost see him yawn tiredly and rub his hand over his face. "Traffic Detail says accident, pure and simple. Finelli was a notorious fast driver. Well, I guess we'll have to leave it at that."

"Can't you even question Everett?"

"About what? About a traffic accident twenty miles from where he lives? They'd scream persecution and they'd be right."

"There might be something in Finelli's notes. His written reports."

"We'll go over them, of course, but it's not likely. There was nothing on his body, by the way, and nothing in the car. But he'd hardly have had time to make any notes if he was following them. If he wasn't, well, that's obvious. And, of course, he could have been following them and still have had an accident through no fault of theirs."

He paused, and I heard him striking a match. Then he went on again.

"It's all a little coincidental, though. That part of 422 runs right along the river and the railroad yards, in the same general area where those tramps got themselves beaten up. You bother me, Sherris. You bring up these things, and more and more they take on the outlines of a nice symmetrical structure. The only trouble is the whole thing hangs in thin air, without one damned infinitesimal fact to support it. And nobody got beaten last night, either."

He sounded really angry.

"Was Finelli a friend of yours?" I asked.

"I knew him around. I wouldn't say a friend, exactly, no. I didn't know him that well. But he was a nice guy. Straight."

"Maybe it was an accident, Pete," I said. "The fellows who investigated ought to know. That's their job."

"Maybe," said Koleski.

There was another pause.

"Accident or not," said Koleski, "if he was trailing the gang and they saw him, they may put two and two together and come after you. You were warned."

"Yeah. But are they likely to connect themselves with the thing that way? I mean, they'd be admitting they knew all about Finelli."

"They wouldn't be admitting anything. Your boy Chuck says he never heard of Everett Bush, and Finelli wrecked his own car. So what's to tie him to that? He could make up any story he wanted to for your benefit. The end result would be the same."

Church bells began to ring faintly at Koleski's end of the line. He yawned again and said, "I'll leave you with that thought. But you be damned careful what you shoot at."

He hung up. It was a beautiful Sunday morning, but for me the good days were over. The shadow had come back.

It was wider this time, and deeper. It had swallowed up Finelli. I had hired a man to do a job, and he had been killed doing it. Accidentally? Deliberately? Or a combination of both? Anyway, the man was working for me, I hired him and paid him. I felt like hell.

Then I got to wondering. I thought about asking Chuck if he would kill me and I remembered his answer. *I might. We haven't tried that yet. We might like it.*

Had they tried it with Finelli?

No, that wasn't their way. They liked to get close to it, to hold it in their hands and feel and taste it. If they ran his car off the road deliberately, it was for necessity, not for pleasure. But was it one of those things where they had realized they were being followed and had wanted to shake him and had done too good a job without really meaning to?

Or had they designedly and with murderous intent forced his car off the road, and then, perhaps, paused long enough to make sure that he was dead?

If so, why?

Why exchange an assault charge, or even several assault charges, for a potential charge of murder?

What had Finelli seen them do?

It was important to know. It was not important to Finelli now but it was to me.

Because, of course, Koleski was right. The boys would learn Finelli's profession from the notice of his death in the paper, and it would take no great effort of mind to figure out who had hired him, and why. They would be angry and they would be afraid, too, because they would not know how much Finelli might have found out about them and passed on to me.

If they hadn't had anything to do with it, and Finelli had been on other business of his own, it didn't matter. But I couldn't believe that.

And if they had murdered Finelli, for whatever reason they found good and necessary, I couldn't see what would hold them back from trying it again with me.

12

We were living under siege again.

This time Tracey refused absolutely to leave me. Her folks came back to town and brought the children with them, and she spent the days with them when I wasn't at home. But in the afternoon after work I would pick her up and we would go back to the house together. We felt safe enough *in* the house. It was the outside, the darkness and the waiting quiet, that were bad.

But it was not so bad now as it had been before. Tracey was with me. She was afraid, and we both knew it, but she was going to stick, and she was so proud of herself, like a little kid that's finally walked the trestle, that I gave up trying to force her to go. I didn't want her to go, of course, for purely selfish reasons. I didn't want any more of those nights alone. I was more worried than I had been before but less scared.

Until something happened. Then it was different.

The rest of Sunday was uneventful. Monday I went downtown on my lunch hour to go over Finelli's report with Koleski. It was in Finelli's office, with that curious feeling of vacuum you get in a place where you have known someone and they have died. The niece cried. There were a couple of other relatives there, packing up books and papers. I felt as guilty as though I had killed him myself. I found out he was married but separated from his wife. I hoped they had been separated a long time, and for her his loss would only be a minor sadness.

There was nothing in the report. Nothing but a neat, meticulous record of a seventeen-year-old boy spending the dullest couple of weeks in his life, going nowhere, speaking to no one.

"Almost too good to be true, isn't it?" Koleski said. "Vacation time, warm nights, a healthy kid. It's not natural."

Nothing about this whole mess is natural," I said. "But it's all negative. I feel as though I'm being smothered with negatives, like the old Chinese torture where they drowned a man in feathers. Still no word of anything happening in the railroad yards that night?"

"Not a peep."

There were three copies of the report, an original and two carbons. I put the original in my pocket and went out with it. It was an expensive trifle. It had cost me some money, but it had cost Finelli more. It weighed on me, the weight of a man's life.

"Did you look at his car?" I asked, as we went down the hall to the elevator.

Koleski shrugged. "No need to. The Traffic lab has been all over it. No signs of impact other than that involved in the accident itself, and not a fleck of foreign paint. He wasn't sideswiped or rammed."

"He was a fast driver, you said."

"On the road, yes."

"But he was a good driver?"

"Nobody's too good to have an accident."

We got into the elevator and clanked slowly down.

"On the other hand," said Koleski, "his car was mechanically in good shape. The road was dry, visibility was perfect, and he must have been over that road and around that curve a million times. That was the way he always drove to and from Newbridge, where his family is. So it's coincidential he should have cracked up there, especially since he hadn't been to Newbridge that night, and that road doesn't go much of anywhere else, unless you're headed straight through to Pittsburgh."

We got out of the elevator.

"His family didn't know anything about what he was doing?"

"No," said Koleski. "Well. See you."

He got in his car and drove away. I sat in mine for a while, thinking. When I did go I drove to Noddy's instead of to the office where I belonged.

It was a slack time there. I sat at the end of the bar and talked to Noddy. I told him how I had hired Finelli and what had happened to him. He was only mildly interested. Then I said, "You never called me."

"About what?"

"Those two guys I wanted to talk to. Harold Francis and the other one, Vorchek."

"Well, I'll tell you," said Noddy. "I couldn't get no place, so what was the use of calling you?"

"Couldn't you locate them?"

"Oh, sure, I asked around. That wasn't too hard. But like I said"—he spread his hands wide—"Francis has been staying with his sister in Mahoningtown since he got out of the hospital. She took care of him, see? And she's one of these God-shoutin' women, won't let anybody near him for fear they'll get him drinking again."

He called her a name or two in whatever language was native to him. "I don't stand on the sidewalk and force 'em in here, do I? Is it my fault if her brother's a lousy white-liner? I don't encourage that kind to hang around. I don't even like 'em in here. But it ain't my fault what they do."

I gathered Francis' sister had blistered his ears for him.

"Vorchek, now," said Noddy, "he's dead."

"Dead?" I straightened up. "How?"

"He didn't have a sister. His friends were so glad to see him back out of the charity ward that they filled him full of cheap wine, and he laid all night in the rain under the East Bridge. Next day he was back in the ward with pneumonia. The end of the week he was in a hole in the ground." Noddy spread his hands again. "So."

"So," I said. "Noddy, is anyone missing since Saturday night?"

"Anybody like who?" His eyes narrowed into that hard jungle look I was beginning to know.

"Just anybody," I said. "Or maybe they're not even missing. Maybe they just got a beating and kept quiet about it, or maybe they didn't even get that. Maybe the boys were scared off."

"The boys again, huh?"

93

"That's what I want to find out."

"But why Saturday? What's with Saturday?"

I told him. He heard me out, getting the point long before I put it into words, watching me with that cold intent stare.

"You know?" he said.

"What?"

"You should of taken your beating and been glad it wasn't worse. You should of forgotten about it."

"Would you?"

"With me it's different. This ain't your kind of a deal."

"Well, it was handed me, anyway. Will you ask around?"

Suddenly he smiled. "I'll ask."

I got Francis' sister's address from him, though he assured me it wouldn't do me any good. Then I called the office and told them I wasn't feeling well and wouldn't be back that afternoon.

I drove to that part of Mall's Ford known as Mahoningtown.

Mahoningtown is railroad. It smells and sounds and tastes of railroad. The soft black soot coats the slate roofs and the clapboards of the old four-roomed houses, lined up side by side on their narrow lots, two rooms up, two rooms down, and a toilet in the cellar. The houses are all the same color. No matter what they were painted, they come out the same uniform dull gray. In some of them women with more time or energy or optimism than their neighbors keep their curtains white. The rest have lost heart. There is a roundhouse and miles of yards. All day and all night the engines chuff and grunt and rumble and shake the ground. All day and all night they talk in their different voices, deep-throated, shrill, mild, querulous, peremptory, pleading, interrupted now and then by the coarse blatting of the Diesels on the through freights and the fast passenger trains. When there's a strike and the road is idle the town dies.

I found the street and the number I wanted and pulled up in front of the house. There was a man sitting in an old swing on the narrow front porch. I walked toward him, up a thin strip of cracked cement between two tiny patches of hard earth with a sprinkling of grass blades on them. He watched me come. He looked clean and well fed. He was wearing a pair of cheap striped cotton pants and a faded blue shirt, with the sleeves rolled

94

up short of the elbows and the collar open. His hair and the stubble on his chin were almost white, but that was not what made him seem old. It was his eyes, pale and empty in a face like a piece of paper someone has crumpled up and thrown away. His hands hung down between his knees. He was not resting. He was not waiting for anything. He was just sitting.

"Are you Harold Francis?" I asked.

He looked at me as a man does through a heavy fog. Perhaps he was trying to remember.

"That's right," he said. "Who are you?"

A woman came out on the porch of the house next door. She peered at me and at my car and went back in again, hurrying.

"I'm Walter Sherris," I told him. "You don't know me, but we have a lot in common. I got beaten up too, before you did."

"Oh," he said, and blinked at my leg. "Is that what happened to you?"

I said it was. There was an old wicker chair by the door. I pulled it up and sat down. Francis put both hands on his body.

"That's where they got me. In the belly. Ain't been right inside since. I tell you, mister. My sister cooks up this slop and I eat it, but I ain't been right. I keep telling her I ain't right. I keep telling her I need medicine, but these goddamn women, they know it all, they won't listen."

He leaned forward, suddenly cunning, his eyes becoming more alert as hope grew up in him.

"Now, you're a man, now, you know how it is. Don't you?"

"Sure," I said, deliberately missing his perfectly obvious point. "I know how it is. I think it was the same gang that beat us both up. Can you remember anything about them, Mr. Francis?"

"They kicked me," he said, putting his hands back on his body again. "Ain't been right since. If I was to get some medicine——"

"How many were there?"

"How many?" He thought about that for some time. The woman next door came out again. She was a very short wide woman in a very clean pink cotton dress. She folded her thick forearms and stood planted by the porch rail, watching.

"Couple of guys," said Francis. He shook his head.

"What do you mean, a couple of guys? Two? Or could there have been more?"

"I was drunk that night," he said, and laughed. "Godawful drunk. I used to be able to drink, mister, I'll tell you."

"But how many were there?"

"Couple. Three. Four. I don't——" He became conscious all at once of the woman on the porch next door. "Goddamned old crow," he said furiously, "she's called my goddamn sister again. I ain't allowed a minute's peace——"

He turned to me. For the moment he looked almost bright, and that was bad, because now his face was no longer pathetic, it was nasty and deceitful, the weak, selfish face of the chronic drunk.

"Listen, mister," he said hurriedly. "I remember a lot. I could tell you a lot of things you want to know. If we was to get in your car and go somewhere, where these goddamned women couldn't interfere, I could tell you. If we was to go before my sister comes——"

He stood up. I glanced past him at the woman on the porch. She made a move as though she would go down the steps, but when I shook my head at Francis and stayed put, she hesitated, poised with one hand on the rail.

"What can you tell me?" I asked. "Were there four or five? Was one big and one short? I don't have a lot of time, Francis. You'll have to tell me now."

He was squinting over my shoulder, down the street. His lips were wet and quivering with eagerness. "If," he said, "you was to give me a little something to buy medicine with, so's I could quiet this pain I got inside——"

I turned and looked too. There was a short gray-haired woman coming up the street, walking fast. She wore a starched white smock over her dress, as though she worked, perhaps, as checker in the small corner grocery.

"I'm afraid I can't do that," I told Francis.

For a moment his eyes were hateful, and then it seemed that he might cry. He sat down heavily in the swing. The gray-haired woman turned in at the walk. She nodded at the woman on the porch next door and called out, "Thank you, Mrs. Barnard."

Mrs. Barnard waved and nodded and remained where she was, watching.

The gray-haired woman approached the steps.

"There she comes," said Francis. "Holy sister Mary. So god-damned holy she couldn't get herself a man." He said it malignantly, making sure she heard. "She's tried all the churches in the book, but they wasn't none of them holy enough for her. I don't know what she'll do now. Start one of her own, I guess."

I stood up, wishing I hadn't come. But Francis' sister paid him no attention. She was looking hard at me, one of those iron, joyless women who seem never to have been young.

"Did you give him any money?" she asked me.

"No," I said.

She was not convinced. "You might think you were doing him a kindness. He's shrewd about getting the drink."

"I didn't," I said. "I just came to ask your brother a few questions," I explained, with those unwelcoming eyes of hers never shifting from my face. "I'm sorry if I've made any trouble for you, but it's important to find out what I can."

She shook her head. "He whines a lot about that beating, but it wasn't that that rotted him inside and out. It was the drink that did it, and he was drunk that night. He doesn't remember anything."

Her tone was calm and matter-of-fact. But it stung Francis into a foggy rage.

"I can remember more than you damn well think," he shouted. "I can remember legs all around me. I remember a great big guy pulled me straight up to my feet and then threw me down again, and another one of 'em laughed. He laughed like a goddamn silly jackass all the time he was kicking my guts out. Don't tell me what I can remember."

"I wouldn't put too much faith in anything he says," his sister told me. "His mind isn't good. Are you ready to go now? I have to get back to my work."

"Aren't you interested in trying to find the boys who beat your brother?"

"No," she said. "The Lord sent them to rebuke him. They

were on the Lord's errand, and the Lord will deal with them as He sees fit."

Francis began to mutter blasphemies. Suddenly he shouted at Mrs. Barnard. "Go on inside, you old crow, the show's over!" His sister spoke sharply to him, and he cursed her. I went out to my car. Just before I drove away I looked up at the house again. They were still on the porch. She was ordering him to go inside and he was refusing to budge, grinning at her in toothless spite. They were happy. You could see it in every line of them, the way they reacted to each other. He had someone to worry and torment, and she had someone upon whom to practice her righteousness, and neither one of them could get away. They were a unit. They belonged.

Koleski was out, but I left a note for him. It seemed beyond doubt to me now that it was the same gang, but cops are harder to convince. I thought he might want to question Francis himself.

I picked up Tracey, stopping long enough to remind the children that they still had a father. "This is a hell of a way to live," I said to my parents-in-law, "but right now I don't know what else to do."

"We love having the children," said Tracey's mother. "Just take care of yourselves, that's all." I knew she had fought it out with Tracey about staying at the house with me and she didn't mention it, but her eyes were dark and deep with worry.

I kissed her and told her not to be afraid. I said I would take care of Tracey, and with the .38 weighing down my pocket it seemed that I ought to be able to. It took only about twenty minutes to remind me of the fact that there are times when a gun is no help.

When you leave North Road on Laurel Terrace Drive you descend almost at once into the gully of a stream bed, paralleling the course of the water for a short distance and then making a fairly sharp left turn across a bridge. You can't take that turn too fast, and on both sides of the bridge the bank is grown thick with scrub willow and rough brush.

I had made my turn onto the bridge and was just starting to pick up speed again when there was a sudden violent *crack!* and something flew past my ear. It hit the windshield. I saw a spider-web pattern spring out like magic on the glass. In the same fraction of a second Tracey said, "Oh!" in a sort of startled, unbelieving way.

She had clapped her hands over her face, and between the fingers I saw a red smear of blood.

13

I TRAMPED on the accelerator.

"Get down," I said to Tracey. "Get down on the floor."

The rear wheels spun and screamed in the scurf of gravel that was always on the bridge, kicked there by passing cars from the berm of the road.

It seemed as though we hung there for an hour, with Tracey sliding down under the cowl, her hands still covering her face, and me with my head pulled down onto my shoulders until my neck hurt with the tension, my foot pressing that damned pedal into the mat.

It could only have been, really, a second or two. Then the car jumped forward. There was another loud noise of something hitting it, but this time lower down, on the rear deck. I looked in the rearview mirror. We were traveling fast now, over the bridge and toward the winding road beyond. I couldn't look long. But I saw a big tall figure come out of the scrub bushes where it had been hidden and stoop and pick up stones and throw them after us, futilely, in a perfect fury of childish exasperation.

Then we had swung around a curve.

"Are you all right?" I asked. "Tracey, baby——"

I was scared. I had never been so scared in all my life.

"I think so," she said, in a weak uncertain voice. She was still huddled under the cowl. I glanced down. She had taken her hands away and was staring at the blood on them. Her eyes were wide.

"It's just a nick," I said. "Only a little nick, honey, right above your eyebrow."

I hoped I was telling the truth.

"Here," I said, and gave her my handkerchief. "We'll be home in a minute. It'll be all right."

She climbed back up on the seat, holding the handkerchief to her forehead. She looked very small. Far too small to be involved in violent happenings.

"What was it?" she whispered.

"I don't know. A bullet. No, I didn't hear any shot." That first loud crack had been when the thing drilled through the back window. There was a hole in it and the glass was all starred. "Never mind," I said. "We're all right now."

I went up that road like a bat out of hell. I was still relatively calm. I hadn't even begun to get it yet. But it's just as well that nothing got in front of me. I had it in my mind to reach home and I don't believe I could have stopped.

I didn't bother with the garage. I whirled into the drive on two wheels, rushed Tracey into the house, and locked the door behind us. I sat her down on the couch and made two phone calls, one to the police and one to Dr. Obermeyer. Then I went back to Tracey.

She was not on the couch. I heard water running in the bathroom. She was washing her face and hands with an almost brutal haste, as though she had to get every drop of blood off them before some important deadline that only she knew about.

"Maybe you better let that alone until Obermeyer comes," I said.

"It's all right, Walt. Just a little nick." She dried her hands and face on a towel, except for the hurt place. She took tissues from a box and patted that, looking in the mirror. "It's already stopped bleeding. It startled me, that's all."

Her lips were white. I was afraid she was going to fall over and I put my arms around her. She smiled at me in the mirror and said again, "It's all right, Walt. Nothing to worry about."

"Come on," I said. "Let's go in the other room and sit down." Suddenly I was afraid I was going to do the falling over. I looked at Tracey in the mirror. "He might have killed you," I said.

"He might have killed you," Tracey whispered. "He tried to. Oh, Walt."

I had a vivid, terrible vision of that missile, whatever it was, hitting me in the back of the head and the car crashing through the flimsy railing of the bridge onto the rocks below, with me dead or senseless at the wheel, and Tracey——

"This ends it," I said. "I don't give a damn who they are or if they're ever caught. We're leaving town. The hell with them. The hell with Valley Steel and this house and all the rest of it. All rolled together they aren't worth you and the kids."

I turned and hurried out of the bathroom, dragging her with me.

"What are you going to do, Walt?"

"Pack."

I pulled her into the bedroom. "There. You sit down on the bed and rest." I kissed her. "You can tell me what you want." I began to pull stuff out of the bureau drawers and throw it in the big chair. Tracey watched me for a minute, holding the wad of tissue to her forehead.

"Walt," she said.

I was busy, hauling stuff out of the drawers and piling it up.

"Walt!"

Her voice was so sharp and strange that I had to look at her. And now she was not pale any more. Her cheeks were blazing and her eyes glittered.

"I'm not going to," she said. "This is my house. They haven't any right. They haven't any right." She repeated that until she choked up and had to stop for breath.

"He hurt me," she said, switching from the general to the particular. "I haven't done anything to him. He nearly killed you, and you haven't done anything to him except try to defend yourself. It isn't right. It isn't just." She began to hammer her two fists on the bed beside her. "You put those things back, Walt. Put them back!"

I was standing with a pile of shirts in my hands, trying dazedly to argue with her, when the doorbell rang. It took me a minute to realize what it was, and then I was afraid again, afraid Chuck had followed and was going to try something new. But the car in the drive was a black sedan with MALL's FORD P.D. painted on the door, and a uniformed policeman was standing by it, looking at the damage to my hard-top. I opened the door.

They were the same two officers who had come before, when the boys tackled me in the yard. I didn't remember their names, if they had told me. Almost before I had the door open a police ambulance arrived and two more men came in, carrying a first-aid box. Tracey said she was all right, but they looked at her anyway, applied antiseptic and a bandage, and said the cut didn't amount to much. They advised me to call our own doctor to prescribe some sedation, and I said I had done that. They went away, and then Dr. Obermeyer and Koleski arrived almost simultaneously. I sent Obermeyer in to Tracey and joined Koleski and the policemen outside by the car. Koleski had another detective with him, a tall bony young fellow named Hartigan. It seemed that he worked with Koleski as a team, but I hadn't happened to meet him before.

One of the cops was doubled over now, poking a flashlight under the front seat of my car. The other one was with Hartigan, examining the dents. They were all listening while I told Koleski what had happened. The Whites and the Thompsons had now come to offer help and find out what was going on, and kids I had hardly ever seen before from all up and down the street were swarming in, bug-eyed with curiosity. I was glad somebody was having fun.

The officer with the flashlight said, "Look here."

Koleski bent over and craned his neck. He grunted. The officer got a long twig and raked at something beneath the seat. He worried it out and into an envelope Koleski was holding. Then he held it out for me to see, and the others gathered round.

It was a round steel ball, the kind they sell for the heavy-duty slingshots that are used for hunting small game.

"At short range," said Koleski, "that could do you plenty of damage. Your wife's lucky she only caught it after it had spent itself. Nice and quiet and not traceable like a bullet—chances are that Chuck figured it and the broken window would be overlooked in the general mess of a wreck, and the thing would be put down as an accident."

"Like Finelli."

"Maybe." He turned to the two cops. "You didn't find anything?"

"Nothing but the trampled place in the bushes where he hid."

Koleski frowned at the metal slug. "I think there'll be another one of these around on the bridge. From your story, and the deep dent on the back there, he fired two of them."

"And then he threw stones." That struck me as very odd, and I said so. "It was such a kiddish gesture, not like Chuck at all. He's always been self-controlled—you know what I mean, where he wanted to be. This time he acted like a child having a tantrum. So damned mad he hadn't killed us, I guess."

I added, "He did another thing that's out of character too. He came right out in the open, in broad daylight. I might have shot him, or another car might have come along. He was taking a chance."

Koleski nodded, as though he too thought that might be important. "And he was alone?"

"There wasn't any sign of anyone else."

The two officers who had checked the scene on their way out agreed with that. The trampled bushes only spoke of one person.

"Well," said Koleski, "Chuck may be having troubles of his own, troubles we don't know about. Let's hope so." He put the envelope in his pocket. "The lab will check this, but I don't think we'll get anything. I'll arrange for a team of men to stake out on your place for a while, just in case."

That relieved me, for the moment, of the necessity to make any decision about going or staying, and I was glad. I was tired. I didn't want to have to think about anything for a while.

Koleski spoke to the cops for a minute, telling them to be on the lookout for a light-colored convertible. Then he said to me, "I got your message about Harold Francis. Either Hartigan or I will talk to him, but I doubt if we'll get any more out of him than you did. I'm amazed you got that much."

"His sister jarred it out of him. It sounds like the same bunch, doesn't it?"

"It sure does. I believe if we could get hold of the stocky kid

104

and make him laugh for us, we'd have all the identifications we want. Everybody seems to remember him."

I said, "I suppose I might have got Chuck today, but my wife was hurt. It didn't seem important."

"You did the right thing," Koleski said.

He left with Hartigan. The cops left. There were still a lot of people around, staring and asking questions. I saw Joe Thompson and asked him please to get them the hell out of there. His wife was in the house with Tracey, and so was Andy White and his wife. Dr. Obermeyer was just leaving.

"The wound is superficial," he said, "but Tracey's had a nasty fright, and from the looks of you, Walter, so have you. I have left four capsules. Give Tracey two of them and take the other two yourself. And give me a ring tomorrow."

I thanked him. He went out, and finally the Whites left too, after we had convinced them there wasn't anything they could do. Both they and the Thompsons were very worked up about it all. It did seem a hell of a thing. As Tracey said, we didn't deserve it. As Tracey said, it wasn't fair.

Nothing more happened that night. We even slept, thanks to Obermeyer's capsules. The next morning Tracey's forehead was puffed up and sore, but otherwise she seemed all right. I sat at the breakfast table watching her move about the kitchen in a flowered housecoat, as pretty as ever except for the patch of white gauze and tape above her eyebrow. It was an obtrusive thing. It stood out. It got bigger and bigger while I watched until I couldn't see anything else.

"Tracey," I said. "I meant that last night. I'm quitting."

This time she didn't flare up at me. She came over and stood beside me, her hand on my shoulder. "You're afraid, aren't you?"

The sunlight fell hot and strong on both of us through the window, but I was cold. "Yes," I said. "I'm afraid."

"So am I. I have been from the first. That was truly the main reason why I wanted you to give up. I know you didn't think so, but it was. I was afraid of what they'd do."

She sat down across from me. "It seems a shame," she said. A flash of the old hot rage came up in me, but the white bandage on Tracey's head cooled it down again fast. It occurred to me to wonder why things had changed with me so suddenly, why fear had come to be more powerful than anger. The obvious answer was that Tracey had been hurt and endangered, and that was true. But there was something more.

Chuck had changed too. He was no longer bent on frightening me or perhaps beating me up again. He was bent on murder.

I had never had anyone come after me before to kill me. It was a new experience. I didn't have any prearranged, preconditioned attitude toward the situation. I didn't have any recommended social behavior to fall back on. I was simply and honestly yellow. There was a cold, cruel, bitter finality about getting murdered that I couldn't quite bring myself to face.

"I was furious last night," Tracey said. She got up and poured coffee and brought the two cups to the table. Her hands shook a little. "But I don't know, this morning I feel different. Tired, I guess. I would like to go away and forget all this. Not to have to worry, worry, worry, every minute."

Her voice had got away from·her. She waited until she could control it again.

"I just don't see," she said, "what we would live on."

"It wouldn't have to be for long. Only until they're caught, or —well, until this thing blows over."

"It's been nearly five months already. Do you know how much we've got in the bank?"

I did, all too well. I drank my coffee slowly, trying to think. It was kind of funny in a way. We had made our gesture of defiance. We had blown our trumpets and waved our banners, and that was that. It was as though we felt we had done all that custom demanded, and the hell with it. Now we were basely considering the safety of our skins.

"We'd get some money from the house," I said. "And maybe George Warren would be able to do something for me. There must be jobs in other towns. We'd make out somehow."

"Dad might help, too, if we needed it. They'd keep the children for us, until we got——"

"No," I said savagely, "the kids go with us. I may have to give up everything else but I'm damned if I give up my family."

Tracey sat and looked gloomily into her coffee, shaking her head.

I said, "It sounds crazy, doesn't it, when you say it right out in words? All because of five boys we never saw or heard of before."

"I guess that's why people like that always have the advantage of people like us."

"How do you mean?"

"Well, they haven't anything to lose, and we do. They don't care what they do to other people, but we care what's done to us. It makes you wonder if they really are human like us, or if they're —I don't know. Throwbacks. Just animals."

"God knows," I said. I didn't feel hungry, and the coffee was sour in my stomach. "Let's get on to town. You can get breakfast there if you want it. Look, why don't you call Mae? She's been wanting to go up to the lake, and it looks like a nice day for it. You could take all the kids, and get your mind off this for a change. Nothing has to be decided today."

She said all right, with a dull lack of interest in the whole thing, but I knew Mae would be good for her. We dressed and rode dismally downtown, with the cracked windshield as a constant reminder.

I told Tracey to tell her folks we'd be staying with them tonight and left her to handle them when they found out why. I didn't think I could face any more talk about any of it just then. I went on to the office.

I didn't do enough work that morning to put in your eye. I kept thinking I ought to go in and talk to George about a job in another town, but I couldn't quite do it. In the first place I didn't think he could or would get me one, and in the second place I didn't want to commit myself—not yet, not quite yet. Maybe tomorrow. Business offices are much like wolf packs. If for any reason you fall off your feet, there are nineteen eager young men with crew cuts waiting to gobble you up and take your place.

I don't know why, but that morning stands out in my mind as the time when I absolutely hit bottom. The chief thing I remember about it is *gray*. Just gray. Everything. Past, present, and future.

I was making an effort to heave myself up to go to lunch with the usual gang when the phone rang on my desk. I answered it. It was a man's voice, gravel-toned and slightly accented.

"Who?" I said, not getting either the name or the voice.

"Noddy. *Noddy.* Ain't this Mr. Walter Sherris?"

"Oh. Sure. Hello."

He came to the point fast. "You asked me to ask around. I did. I think I got something. Maybe."

"What?" I asked, excited in spite of myself.

"I ain't sure. Listen, how's your guts, friend? Pretty strong?"

"I—guess so. Why?"

"Drop by here about seven-thirty, eight o'clock. I'll show you some life you ain't seen before, and we can incidentally hang our ears out in the breeze. Okay?"

I was going to say no, and if he knew anything he should go to the police with it, and if he didn't he should forget it. I was going to say I was all through with that.

But I didn't.

I said yes.

14

I⊤ was a sultry evening, still light, but banking up that familiar blackness in the west. It had been one long blazer of a heat wave and apparently it was going on right into fall.

I left the car on the nearest lot and walked down to Noddy's. I had called the house. Tracey had not come back yet from the lake, but Dad was there. He said they had been dreadfully upset by what had happened, and he had sent Mother up too for the day. Mae had been upset too, he said, and I said I knew she was because she had tongue-lashed me for twenty minutes over the phone, winding up with an invitation for me and Tracey and the kids to move in with them for a while.

"She's a great girl," Dad said. "I've always liked her."

"She's the best. Listen, Dad, I may be late tonight. I've just heard from a fellow—I don't know whether it'll come to anything or not, but it's sort of a last chance. Nothing dangerous at all. Tell Tracey not to worry, and I've got a key."

"I'll probably be up when you come in, Walt," he said. "I'm a late reader, you know. Be careful."

I assured him I would be. And I intended to be. I still had the .38 in my pocket. I wondered, not for the first time, what I would do if the time ever came to use it. Handling guns on a rifle range is one thing. Using them with intent to kill is another. How do you feel, a peaceable citizen with no leanings toward violence, when you face another man—or a boy, even worse, a boy with no beard yet to his chin and no real knowledge, in spite of his crimes, of this life you are going to take away from him—how do you feel when you face him and choose your spot and fire? Do you look into his eyes and recognize him as a human being, or do you know him only as a blind agency of evil, a menace, a thing to be stamped out and made not? I didn't know, and I didn't want to know. I hoped I would not be forced to find out.

Noddy's was already lively with the early-evening trade. I saw Miller in one of the booths and went over and talked to him for a minute, telling him how it had gone with the Bush boy.

"I still think he's the boy," I said.

He nodded. He had a newspaper spread out on the table in front of him. "You see this?"

I said I had. Somebody on the police beat had picked up the story of yesterday's attack, and because of what had gone before he was able to make quite a little thing out of it. "I'll be famous," I told Miller, "if I live long enough."

"And the famouser you get, the more the gang will be afraid of getting caught," said Miller. "I was you, mister, I wouldn't go down any dark alleys without I had a friend walking behind me."

"Believe me," I told him, "I won't."

"You ready?" said Noddy's voice over my shoulder. I turned around. He was wearing green slacks and a striped sport shirt. "Sharp," said Miller. "Sharp!"

Noddy frowned at me. "We might get into some rough walking. Can you make it?"

"I can make it."

"Don't lose him," said Miller to Noddy, and grinned. "He's okay."

We went past the bar, where another man was serving, and through a curtained doorway into a back hall, and down that to a big room stacked high with stale-smelling cases of empty beer bottles. Noddy's car was parked outside the back door, in a narrow alley made all of damp bricks, one of those places that the sun has never managed to get into since it was built.

"I got two jugs in the back," he said. "Vino. Cheap. We're all set."

We got into the car. "What are we after?" I asked. "Can't you tell me?"

He shook his head. "So far I got a word, that's all. Just a word. And a word ain't nothing unless you got more to go with it." He shrugged. "Maybe we get more, maybe we just spend a hot evening getting winoed."

He drove to the mouth of the alley and waited his chance to make the dive into traffic. I looked at him.

"You're going to a lot of trouble for me," I said. "I'm grateful. But I don't see why."

"Well," said Noddy, "it's like this. I don't like them boys either. And if they're doing what we think they're doing they oughta be stopped. Right?"

"Right."

"So," he said, "I got possibly a source of information. It's no good to the cops. It's no good to you. It's only good to me."

He leaned over the wheel, measuring the distance between a westbound steel truck and an eastbound tanker. He added, "Maybe I like the way you fight, mister." And he stepped on the gas.

We made it.

"I'm sorry to disillusion you," I said, "but this is my last stand. If we don't come up with something definite tonight, I'm through."

"I read the paper," Noddy said. "Your woman is all right, huh?"

I said she was.

"But you're scared now."

"I am."

"Well, there's nothing wrong with that. When I hear a man say he ain't afraid of anything, I figure he's either a half-wit or a liar. Fear's a good thing. Without it you're dead. You know? I think all these yap-heads you read in the papers are crazy."

"Which ones?" I asked.

"These dames and such that tell you how you should raise your kid. Never frighten 'em. Teach 'em everybody's their friend and the world's as soft as a marshmallow. So what good does that do 'em? It ain't true. I got a boy fifteen. I took him down to the Receiving Hospital once on a Saturday night. I let him watch. I tell him that's what happens to guys who drive too fast. I took him around the jail. I tell him that's what happens to guys who get in trouble with the law. I show him the drunks and the hopheads, and I tell him that's what happens to guys who go on the booze or start shooting the dream-dust. So he's scared witless. He's scared to drive too fast, he's scared to get in trouble, he's scared to drink or take dope. This is bad?"

I didn't think it was bad at all. I said I would remember to do that with Pudge when he was older.

Noddy grinned. "Remember something else too."

"What's that?"

He held up his hairy, powerful right hand. "Best teacher in the world still. Let the woman scream all she wants to. Use it."

We had been heading east with the black clouds towering up behind us hiding the sun. Now Noddy crossed the river on the Smith Street bridge, over the railroad yards, where you can look westward down the winding line of mills and factories, ugly monstrosities foul with smoke, that make the wealth of Mall's Ford. I looked west in the glimmering stormy twilight. Then I looked east, and in the distance along a bend of the multiple tracks I saw the lunar peaks of a strip mine. And I thought of Finelli, who had died just along the road a piece from that mine, and I began to sweat between sudden hope and fear of disappointment.

Noddy made a hairpin turn across traffic at the end of the bridge and slid down an almost perpendicular street that angled to the bottom of the valley, riding the brake and bounding in and out of the holes in the old brick pavement. There were houses on both sides of the street, packed tight together, frame houses with slate roofs and tumbling porches, black with perhaps eighty years of railroad soot. Some of them were empty, the lower windows boarded, the upper ones without glass, wide open to the wind and rain. Others were still inhabited. You could hardly say lived in.

At the foot of the street was a dump, one of those haphazard and illegal middens, fanning out into coarse grass. Noddy skirted the edge of this and went jouncing out over a barely discernible track that might once have been used by wagons, heading back now toward the bridge. There was a house there, almost lost in the shadow of the steel-and-concrete piers. It probably had been a farmhouse, back in the days when this rich bottom land still grew corn instead of slag and railroad ties. Now it was nothing. It was not even a house, really. It was just a forgotten thing that nobody had bothered to tear down.

There were people in it.

Noddy stopped the car. "Let me do the talking," he said. "You're just a pal I brought along and you had an accident. And don't try to hold up your end with these birds. I don't know what kind of a head you've got for vino, but it ain't enough. Okay?"

"You're the boss," I said.

We got out. Noddy took one of the jugs from the back and locked the car carefully. Then we walked toward the house. Traffic rumbled over the high bridge. A switch engine hooted in the yards, and there was a long rattling crash, several times repeated, of empty cars being humped into motion. It was almost dark. Four men came to meet us, scuffing through the tin cans that littered the ground outside their door.

Noddy introduced them. Suby, Cotter, Jellyhead, Sligh. In the dim light their faces were indistinct. Some were taller and some were shorter, but they all had the same hunched-over, tucked-up look, their shirts and their shapeless pants hanging on them as on figures made of broomsticks. Most of them seemed to have gray hair, but whether they were young or old I could not tell, even by their voices.

"We thought you was the cops. Hey, Noddy, whatcha got there?"

"Sonofabitch threw me out last time I was in his place. Didn't you, Noddy? Sonofabitch."

"So I got a business to run, Jellyhead. No hard feelings. Look what I brought."

"Free? For nothing?"

"For nothing. The good red vino." He shook the jug. "Let's have a party."

"Hey," said the one called Cotter suspiciously. "How come you're all of a sudden so generous? You don't give nothin' away free."

"The hell I don't. How many times did you sleep in my back room, huh? And how many times I've stood you to a drink when you was sick and didn't have the price?"

"*One* lousy drink," said Jellyhead, still standing on his hurt pride.

"Okay," said Noddy. "Okay." He turned around. "Come on, pal. We'll go drink our jug somewheres else."

Immediately they caught hold of him, and Cotter turned and kicked Jellyhead.

"Shut up your ugly mouth," he told him. "What the hell do we care, anyway? It's wine, ain't it? And it's free, ain't it?"

Noddy looked at me. "Well, what do you say, pal? Shall we stay?"

"Sure," I said. "Why not?"

Noddy went up to the house and sat down on the ground with his back against the wall. I sat beside him on the flat slab of stone that made the doorstep. The door behind me was half open on one hinge as though it had stuck there, and I doubted if it could be shut at all. It was pretty dark inside, but light enough to see furniture if there was any. There wasn't, beyond a few boxes and a frowsy litter of stuff on the floor. A sour smell came out of mice and rot and damp plaster. I wondered what on God's earth would make a man willing to live this way, and then I saw how the four of them had crouched down in a ring around Noddy, watching him take the cork out of the jug. You could almost see their eyes glitter and their tongues hang out, and I thought of Harold Francis, clean and well fed and comfortable and hating every minute of it, yearning to get back to this.

I still didn't understand.

The jug went around. Nobody bothered about glasses. I doubt if there were any. You drank and swiped the mouth of the jug with your hand or your shirt sleeve, as a ceremonial gesture, before you passed it on. We sat in the warm evening, and it got dark, and all the lights of the city were on, distant enough to be pretty without intruding on us. Traffic on the bridge slacked off. On the hill behind us there was a radio going, and a baby cried, a thin penetrating screech. It was a shocking sound. At least it was shocking to me, to think of any child born and brought up in those ratholes. Somebody, I thought, ought to come with flame throwers and antiseptics and scrubbing brushes, and clean out these black places in the city, open them up and let the sun in. We ought to be ashamed of ourselves, I thought, to allow places like this to stand year after year and not do anything about them.

At first I just tilted the jug up without really drinking, but after a while the whole business began to get on my nerves. I took two or three pulls on the raw sour stuff, trusting to the alcohol to fight off the germs, and that didn't seem to do any good, so I took two or three more. The men squatted on the ground, smoking our "tailor-mades" greedily, blobby figures in a dim canvas. Their voices were meaningless, a monotonous blabber of obscenity and pointless gossip. They were laughing a lot now, getting cheerful, having a good time. I began to be angry with Noddy for bringing me here. The clouds banked so heavily in the west had begun to throw lightning around. The thunder rumbled. I thought the storm was moving north and that we would not get any rain from it here and I was glad. I did not want to be forced to take shelter in that house.

Noddy got up. I started to get up, too, because I wanted very much to go away from there, but he pushed me down, hard.

"Never mind," he said. "I'll get it."

He went to the car and came back with the other jug, and it started all over again. I knew I had better be careful, but it was too much to expect a body to take this cold sober. I shared the jug again. The red and green and yellow eyes of the block signals shone. I watched the pattern shift and heard the rails begin to hum, and then a train roared through with that particular magic that trains have, a rush of wheels and a flashing of bright windows on the night, and a hoarse wild echo dying.

"—they beat up Harry Francis," Suby was saying. "Sure I did. I was crossin' the yards down there and I seen these guys."

"What guys?" asked Cotter. "Let's have all the goddamn details, pal. All of 'em."

"What do you care so much?" said Jellyhead, thrusting his chin forward.

"Someday," said Cotter, "I'm gonna write a book."

Nobody laughed.

"How the hell do I know what guys," said Suby. "It was dark. I heard 'em coming along, laughing. I ducked back behind a string of cars and waited till they was gone. You bet!"

I was sitting up straight on my doorstep now. But Noddy was carrying the ball, and I had sense enough to let him.

"Hell, Suby," he said, "you're a big strong guy. What was you so scared of?"

"Listen," said Suby, on a high note of indignation. "I heard about these guys. They been around all summer. They beat up ol' Stef Vorchek. That night I saw 'em they just beat up on Harry Francis. I didn't want to have nothin' to do with 'em."

"Aw," said Noddy. "Pass that jug around, boys. I gotta wash that down."

Suby was getting mad now. "A'right," he said. "A'right. You ask anybody in the jungle. They'll tell you."

"Is that right?" asked Noddy, looking at Sligh and Cotter.

"I guess so," said Sligh, shrugging his shoulders. "I never seen 'em myself, but word's kind of got around. Seems like there's this gang of young punks come down to have a little fun, and they never bother the sober guys or if you're with a bunch. But if you're real loaded, see, and by yourself—*boom!*"

"Hey," said Suby abruptly. "Hey, you know what?"

"What?"

"I'll bet they got Artie Clymer."

Noddy moved beside me in the dark, just a little, and I knew that Artie Clymer was the word he'd been waiting for.

15

N<small>ODDY</small> leaned forward, passing the jug.

"Who got Artie Clymer?" he demanded. "What about Artie? Listen, I got a personal interest in that boy. He owes me money. He better not be gone."

"Well, he ain't been back for three days," said Suby. "A guy doesn't just go off and not come back for three days."

Noddy laughed rudely. "Tell me," he said. "I've known you not to come back for three weeks if you latched onto a supply somewheres."

"Maybe so," said Suby, with a certain dignity, "but that's different. Artie was bunking with us, so I know. He didn't go away. He went to the strip mine."

"Whatcha mean, he went to the strip mine?"

"Just what I said, he went to the strip mine. He——" Suby stopped to attend to the jug, and Cotter took up the story.

"Company just finished pulling out of there that day. When was that, Sligh? Sunday? What the hell you talking about, Sunday! What's today?" He did some figuring on his fingers. "Saturday, that's when. Saturday night, and we were doing good. Artie was drunk as a hoot owl. He said that ol' strip mine was just busting with stuff laying around, and he was gonna get it before somebody else did. So he picked up a sack and took off." Cotter made an expressive gesture with his hands. "And that's all."

"Well, didn't you look for him?" Noddy demanded.

"Oh, sure. Next day or so, when he didn't come back. We couldn't find him, and nobody else seen him, either. We even asked the junkman where we take all our stuff. He never was there, this time."

"You know what?" said Suby in a hushed voice. "I bet ol' Artie's laying in a ditch somewheres right now, stone-cold dead."

"Aw, hell," said Noddy. "Sonofabitch owes me money. I'm gonna look for him."

He got up and pulled me to my feet. "Come on, pal, we're gonna look for Artie. I'll get the flashlight out of the car."

"Sure," said Suby. "Sure. Let's all go look for poor ol' Artie."

We went straggling out in an uncertain line, among the tin cans and the empty jugs.

"Hell with'm," muttered Jellyhead. But he came too, grumbling.

We looked for Artie Clymer, in the hot night, with the thunder booming and the lightning flaring in the north, and people all over Mall's Ford watching television or going to the movies or sitting on their porches holding hands. I was looking for Artie Clymer in dank ditches choked with weeds and refuse, under stacks of railroad ties smelling strong and clean of creosote, beside the gravel bank where the highway ran, Route 422, where another man named Finelli had met his end on that same Saturday night.

"What about these five guys?" asked Noddy. He was keeping close to me, giving me a hand now and then over the roughest spots. "You saw 'em, Suby. What were they like?"

"I told you it was dark. I couldn't see what they looked like."

"You said they were laughing?"

"Yeah. Yeah, they were laughing. Give me the creeps, you know what I mean? Like they done an evil and was glad of it. Specially one of 'em. Haw, haw, haw—God! Like an animal."

My insides were tight as a bowstring, but I kept my mouth shut and waited.

"Five of 'em," said Noddy.

"Yeah. But the four of 'em was picking on the other guy. At least it seemed that way."

"Picking on him?"

"You know, kind of hustling and pushing him around, like,

118

and needling him. Now wait a minute, don't rush me. I'm thinking. One of 'em said something like, You wanta be on the top with us, or on the bottom like him? Something like that. Like they were threatening this guy."

We had reached the entrance to the strip mine now, a blank mouth of desolation gaping in the night.

Cotter said suddenly, "Hey, look at this."

Noddy swung the beam of his flashlight over were Cotter was standing. We all moved together in a clump, looking down. There was a stand of stiff dead weed there, and mingled with it were a gunny sack and an old cloth cap.

Suby sniffled. "Poor ol' Artie," he said. "That there's his own old cap, and the sack he took with nothin' in it."

"Looks to me," said Cotter, "like he never made the strip mine."

Noddy turned his head and said slowly, "I kind of think you're wrong, Cotter. I kind of think he did."

Nature, in some localities, has provided shallow seams of coal, so that men with large machines can dig them quite easily from the surface. The machines tear up the trees and the grass, the sod and the topsoil, the clay and the gravel, and pile them in that order in little conical mountains ranged on either side of the seam, so that when they get through they have made a perfect minia-ture copy of a valley on the moon, and this is called a strip mine. They used to just go away and leave them when the coal was all dug. If you took the old shuttle flight from Mall's Ford to Pittsburgh you would fly over a practically endless chain of these gray-white areas where no blade of grass could possibly ever grow until geological ages transformed the clay and gravel again into topsoil. Then I guess somebody got alarmed, and a law was passed. Now the machines have to level down the hills and fill the pits and replace the soil and seed it.

In this particular mine the coal digging was finished and the leveling off had not begun.

We went in over the broad access, past the rusty steel cable that kept cars out, past the Private Property-Keep Out signs and the Danger-No Trespassing signs. Me limping and four drunken scarecrows, with Noddy the only man among us that looked capable of dealing with anything, lurching and staggering in the fitful dark over the flint-hard beaten ruts of a million truck wheels, down the wide sloping valley between the conical peaks. A wind had begun to blow off the storm to the north. It lifted my hair and set my shirt to flapping. It felt good but it made the darkness and the uncertain footing more confusing. Noddy's light stabbed here and there. A little way ahead I saw the gleam of water, one of those dank pits full of seepage and runoff that children sometimes drown themselves in. There were lumps of coal scattered underfoot, and occasionally a bit of broken iron or some other useless thing thrown away, treasure-trove, I suppose, to a man like Artie Clymer.

Noddy grunted suddenly and stopped. His flashlight steadied on a small object. Again we all clustered around and stared. This time it was a shoe.

We found the mate to it perhaps ten feet farther on. The men swore they were Artie's. He had picked them up out of a trash can, they said, and they were too big for him, so that they might easily have fallen off. Jellyhead started to pick them up, but Noddy stopped him.

We went on, moving slower now, down the slope toward the pit. It was roughly square, perhaps forty feet across and Lord knew how deep. As deep as the coal pocket had been. It seemed awfully cold even on that hot night, the surface riffling very faintly in the wind, as though the lead-colored water was as heavy as it looked.

"*Look* out!" said Noddy sharply. "Damn you, Sligh, you're tramping all over it. Move over. Yeah, you too. Now stand still a minute." He hunkered down, switching the light back and forth till he got an angle that suited him. "You see that, Sherris?"

The ground was looser here close to the pit where the trucks had not pounded it down. There were marks in it, smoothed but not effaced by the wind. Sligh came and breathed on the back of my neck and we considered them together, with Suby and Cotter and Jellyhead bending over Noddy.

"Something's been dragged," I said.

The beam of the flashlight followed the marks, and our heads followed the light. On the very edge of the pit the dirt was churned and dented, as though by heels dug into it during a period of effort.

"God," said Cotter almost gently. "Do you think——"

Noddy grunted. "We better leave it right here." He straightened up. "Don't go no closer, you're liable to trample out some evidence."

He made them go off to the side where the trucks had been, where nothing would show anyway. Then he and I started working our way back slowly toward the entrance, treading as on eggshells, his flashlight twitching this way and that like the fading lightning. One of the men, perhaps it was Suby, seemed to be sobbing.

We found what we were hunting for close to where that first shoe lay capsized in a rut, its broken sole turned to the sky. This was back on the flinty ground, but even so you could squint and find the scratches, the scrapes and gouges, the kicked-up pebbles.

You could see another thing, now that you were expecting it. You could see a spattering of dark stains on the light yellow clay. They might have been spilled oil, but you knew they were not. Even at night you knew that.

"Well," said Noddy at last, "let's go call 'em."

"Call who?" asked Jellyhead.

"The cops, stupid. Who the hell else?"

"Cops," said Jellyhead. "Oh, no. I won't have no part of no cops."

Noddy went over to him and took the front of his shirt in a bunch in one hand. He shook him, just once, very hard. Jellyhead did not protest. Noddy said slowly and distinctly so that they all could hear,

"Artie Clymer's laying dead in that pit there. Somebody dragged him in here and beat him up and threw him in. That's murder. When there's a murder you got to call the cops."

"I didn't have nothing to do with it," said Jellyhead, showing his teeth.

"Well, you got something now," said Noddy. "Cotter, you got more sense than the others. You know how it'll look if any of you guys run away. It'll look like you were maybe in on it.

You keep 'em here till I get back and you got nothin' to worry about. Okay?"

"Okay," said Cotter doubtfully.

"You and your free wine," growled Jellyhead. "I knew there was a catch in it somewheres."

Noddy gave him another shake. "You, Jellyhead," he said. "You're the stupidest sonofabitch in the whole damn jungle. Listen. I'll tell you something. If these guys that killed Artie ain't caught they'll be back after another sucker, and how do you know it won't be *you* laying under the cold water next time?"

Jellyhead snorted and pulled himself free but he sat down on a rock at the edge of the truckway. The others, Suby and Sligh, were looking back at the glimmering pit, swaying slightly in the wind as they stood. Cotter was rubbing nervously at his chin, rasping the bristles and cursing almost inaudibly. Noddy looked at me.

"Coming?"

"No," I said. "I'll stay here."

He seemed doubtful. "I can go faster without you," he said, "but I don't——"

"I'll stay." I had a feeling our four scarecrows would melt away into the night if they weren't watched, in spite of Noddy's threats. I had my gun if I needed it. And I had done enough walking for a while.

"There's a garage about a half a mile down the highway," said Noddy. "I can phone from there. It won't take long."

He went off up the slope at a fast trot. I found myself a rock not too close to the one Jellyhead was sitting on. The wind had dropped and the storm was rumbling off toward the east. I lighted a cigarette and gave the rest of the pack to the others to shut them up and then I turned, like Suby, to look at the still water of the pit.

I thought, That's what they did that night. That's why they had to kill Finelli.

That's why Chuck tried to kill me, so that I wouldn't do what I have just, with Noddy's help, done.

And they're just kids, I thought, my God. Just kids.

I felt sick. The sour wine turned in my stomach and the smoke of the cigarette tasted bad. I threw it away.

I wondered how it had happened. The boys had been pretty careful so far. They had not beaten any of the four other men as badly as they had me, and me they had tackled in hot blood, in anger and frustration. The others they had done with a certain restraint, a judicious knowledge of when to quit. Chuck had threatened to kill me that night in the garden, but it was only a threat, and he had a reason—if anybody ever has a reason. I was trying to get to him. Artie Clymer wasn't. Why did they kill him? For the fun of it? Or by accident, that almost inevitable accident that I remembered having mentioned once to Koleski?

The air was hot again, stale and heavy now that the wind was gone. I sat hunched over on my rock, staring at the blank earth, and I thought I could see how it had been. The scuffling, the swaying back and forth, the blind minute of pleasure as old and dark and primitive as night, and then the sudden silence. One blow too hard, one blow too many, and now it was not pleasure, it was death. I thought I could see that swift flare of panic and then the hurried frantic effort to hide what had been done, to cover it up and go away, pretending it had never happened.

And then they had realized they were followed, and not all the lies in the world would do them any good.

The journey begins with a single step, but once you have taken it you can't turn back, and every precipice you come to is steeper and darker and more cruel than the last one, but you can't turn back.

I wondered where Chuck's next precipice would be.

16

An hour later the place was swarming with people and Artie Clymer was getting more attention than he ever had when he was living. Floodlights had been set up. Areas of dirt had been carefully fenced off and men were busy at them with cameras and scrapers and *moulage* kits. Another crew, grotesque fishermen beside a ghastly pond, were casting grapnels into the water, and drawing them, and moving, and casting again.

Koleski was standing beside me with Hartigan. He was smoking and looking blue, and I didn't blame him. This call had dragged him from a pleasant date with his girl and it was nothing to exchange for it. Hartigan was grumpy too. He'd been home with his family. There was a man from Homicide down by the pit, talking to the lab men. There was also a man from Juvenile. The boys between them were spreading out now to involve the whole police department.

"They haven't found anything yet," I said, looking at the crew with the grappling hooks.

"They just started. Give them time," Koleski said.

"Suppose they don't? I mean—suppose we're wrong."

"There's something in there. Chances are it's a body," Koleski threw down his cigarette and stepped on it, although there was nothing in this place to burn. "They may not find it for hours. No reason for you to hang around anyway. I'll let you know."

"Yes," I said. "Noddy'll be back with the car in a minute. That's what I'm waiting for."

The man from Homicide came up. His name was Quinn. He was older than Koleski and harder-looking, a short dark powerful man with grizzled patches over his ears.

"They got a couple of fair heelprints," he said. "Might be useful. Good thing it hasn't rained since Saturday."

He looked at me. "All the signs point to it, mister, and if we do turn up a body I'd like to talk to you myself. There's a lot of background on this case I don't savvy yet."

"There's a lot of it we don't savvy either," said Koleski. "It's one of those damn senseless things. No motive. Well, obviously there's a motive, but you know what I mean. No *reason* to it. And no witnesses. Not one single loving witness. They like it dark and they like it quiet and so far they've been luckier than they deserve." He added with cynical impatience, "Assuming of course that the same gang did this."

"You heard Suby's story?" I asked. "About meeting them in the freight yard?"

"I did. I believe it. I believe they probably killed this tramp —what's his name, Artie something?—and tossed his body in the hole to hide it. I believe that Finelli either saw them do it, or more likely saw them come in here, or come out, or both, but in any case would have been able to place them here definitely at that time, and would certainly have investigated to see what they were up to if he didn't already know. I believe they spotted him and ran him off the road. And all that means, of course, that I believe he was trailing Everett Bush, and that therefore Bush is one of the gang."

He shrugged. "Maybe Quinn can prove it. I haven't been able to get a handhold anywhere."

"But this is different," I said. "You can question the Bush boy now, can't you?"

"Sure," said Koleski. "We can question him. We will question him. And if he's got sense enough to keep his mouth shut, we haven't got a thing on him and you're liable to get sued for hounding him with a detective."

"You sound kind of defeated, pal," said Quinn, grinning.

"I hoped it wouldn't come to this," Koleski said.

We looked for a moment without speaking at the glaring lights and the neat efficient bustle of men working at the business of murder.

"Yeah," said Quinn. "I know what you mean. Kids. It's nasty."

"Something new around here," said Hartigan. "That's big-city stuff. Mall's Ford must be growing."

Koleski shook his head. "I don't think this has anything to do with towns or cities. I don't even think it has too much to do with juvenile delinquency. This is a matter of the individual."

"It always is, isn't it?" said Quinn. "When you come right down to it. I mean, it's the individual neck that gets stretched."

I shivered. Suddenly I was afraid I wouldn't get out of there before they found the body and I had an idea I might do something disgraceful like vomiting in front of these policemen. I had never met Artie Clymer and I didn't want to meet him now. His old pals of the can-gang were gone, an unhappy crew being ridden down to Headquarters for interrogation, and not much cheered by Noddy's promises of free jugs. I was glad when I saw Noddy's gaudy shirt in the distance, coming my way.

I made sure Koleski had the address and phone number. He seemed relieved that we had abandoned our house for the time being.

"The regular patrols are keeping an eye on your place, in case somebody shows up there. But I'd feel better with you somewhere else, that's for sure. Particularly after this business breaks in the news. This is probably exactly what Chuck was afraid of."

"By that time," I said, "we may have Chuck where we want him."

"I hope so," said Koleski, without any conviction. "Anyway, Walt, just go on home to bed and don't do us any more favors tonight. Huh?"

"I promise."

Koleski shook his head. "I hate to see you coming. And it's too bad. I think I'd have liked you if I'd met you any other way."

"Sorry," I said. We shook hands, and I said good night to Hartigan and to Quinn, who looked as sharp as an old dog fox. I went off with Noddy.

I was glad to get into the car and rest after bucketing around over all that rough ground and perching on stones. We passed the curve where Finelli went off. There was a tree broken short where his car had hit it, the sharp stump still white and new. In daylight you would see a long sliding scar down the steep bank to the bottom. Noddy said, "I could use a couple shots myself. How about you?"

"No more of that vino. Gah!"

"Were you drinking that stuff? I told you."

"Yeah. Well, your hunch paid off. Hadn't been for you, they'd probably never have found Artie Clymer."

Noddy grunted. He drove for a while without speaking. Then he said, "Artie was no-good. All those guys are no-good. I don't love 'em. But this is wrong. You know? It ain't natural. Now if Jellyhead or Cotter had knocked his brains in over a bottle of booze or a dollar's worth of scrap iron, I wouldn't turn a hand. But this ain't natural."

"No," I said. "It's not. I get to wondering sometimes——"

"What?"

"Well, if they hadn't found me that night, just at the psychological moment. If they hadn't discovered then that beating somebody up was an outlet for everything that bothered them, if they hadn't found out they liked it. Would they have done these other things?"

"Sure they would," said Noddy. "Hadn't been you, it would have been another guy, another time. You ever have a no-good dog? He's maybe got brothers and sisters that are fine as silk, but he's no good. No matter how hard you work with him, he's still no damn good. He was born that way. Don't let 'em kid you people ain't, too."

He turned into the alley and we were back again.

I sat in the car a minute, too tired to get out. I remember Noddy looking in at me from his side, in the dim light that shone from over his back door.

I said, "I don't care."

"What don't you care?" he asked.

"I don't give a damn why they did it, or what they want that they haven't got. I don't see that it matters one damn little bit. I'm just as—as messed up. Artie Clymer's just as dead, and neither one of us is responsible for any of it. I don't care why. I only care about whether they're going to get away with it."

"Come on," said Noddy. "Let's get those drinks."

We had them, and then I got my car and drove home, or rather to where Chuck and his pals had forced me to take refuge. Dad was still up, and so was Tracey, looking very woebegone and worried. The fate of Artie Clymer didn't seem like a cheerful bedtime story, but they pressed me so hard to know what had happened that I gave them a brief run-down, adding that of course they hadn't found the body yet, so it might be all a mistake.

Dad said, "But you don't think it is?"

"No. And the police didn't, either."

"And you're sure now that they killed the detective?"

"I haven't a doubt."

Dad shook his head. He was one of those gentle people to whom violence is as incomprehensible as it is upsetting.

"Dreadful," he said, and shook his head again. "Dreadful. Surely they can make that boy confess now."

"I hope so, Dad," I said. "I hope so!"

I went to bed and dreamed of leaden water under a dark sky. I made a journey down a dead valley where a wind blew and a nameless thing pursued me, always out of sight. I hid under the leaden water, and it was cold, and the thing fished for me with three-pronged claws like grappling hooks.

Around eight in the morning Quinn called. They had found the body. It had been identified as the body of Artie Clymer. There had not been an autopsy yet, of course, but the police surgeon said there was no doubt the man had been beaten. They wanted me to come down.

I asked Tracey to call the office for me and explain why I wouldn't be in. Then I went down to Headquarters, in the hot bright morning.

Quinn met me in one of the interrogation rooms. He had a sheaf of typewritten sheets on the table in front of him, reports on the case so far that Koleski had given him. There was a police stenographer, a young fellow with pad and pencil in front of him and his mind on the world outside the grimy window, where there were fishing and pretty girls.

Koleski and Hartigan were out getting Everett Bush, to bring him in again for questioning.

Quinn went through the papers methodically. He said he was pretty well filled in on the background, but there were still a few questions he wanted to ask. He asked them, and I answered, and the stenographer wrote them down. I kept looking at the door, waiting for Koleski to come in.

It must have been close on to two hours before he did. He was alone. He sat down at the end of the table and took his hat off and lit a cigarette. He didn't say anything.

Quinn asked, "Did you get him?"

"No."

Quinn waited. I shut my teeth hard on my tongue and waited too.

Koleski said, "He's in Cincinnati. With his parents. They're visiting her mother."

"Oh," said Quinn. "When did they leave?"

"Crack of dawn on Sunday morning. We checked it out with the neighbors."

Quinn said, "What about Saturday night?"

Koleski looked at me. "How are you this morning, Walt?"

"Go on," I said, "get it over with."

"Well," said Koleski, "the way we had it figured out, Finelli followed Everett Bush, and through him the whole gang. He could have put the finger on them, as we say, or the Clymer thing, and so they felt compelled to get rid of him as the only witness. Right?"

"Right," I said. "One, two, three."

"Yes," said Koleski, "only we do not have 'one' any more, which leaves two and three hanging in mid-air, looking silly."

He looked from me to Quinn and back again.

"Somebody killed Clymer, and Finelli certainly died, but whoever did it and however it happened, two things are abolutely sure. Everett Bush had nothing to do with it, and Finelli was not following him. He couldn't have been, because Everett Bush did not go anywhere. He never left the house on Saturday night."

17

I DIDN'T say anything at all for a minute. Quinn carefully gathered all the report sheets together in the folder and closed it.

"In that case," he said, "it looks like I've got a body, but nothing more."

I said, "Don't get sore at me, Pete, but I've got to ask you. Are you sure? His parents lied for him once before."

"Maybe they did, maybe they didn't. We don't know for sure. But this isn't his parents. This is his aunt and uncle. They spent Saturday evening with the Bushes. I got this from the next-door neighbor and I went to a lot of trouble to run it down. It's authentic. I've been doing this kind of thing for years, Walt. Believe me."

"All right," I said. "I've already apologized."

"Auntie had a lot of messages to send to Mama," Koleski said, as though he was determined to leave me no saving shred of doubt. "They stayed till after eleven. Both aunt and uncle state positively that Everett was there every minute. They remember particularly because there was a big row about it."

"Row?" said Quinn.

"Yeah. Everett wanted to go out, and his parents wouldn't let him. They were leaving early for Grandma's and they wanted him in bed at a reasonable hour. I guess Everett's language was scandalous, and the old man whacked him. He stayed in. He might have sneaked out after they left, I suppose, but that wouldn't do us any good. Artie Clymer was already on his way to the mine by then. So that's that."

"Well," I said, getting up, "I guess you don't need me any more."

"No," said Koleski, "I guess not."

Quinn said, "Thanks for the body."

"With my compliments. Have fun."

"I'll let you know," Koleski said, "if anything new turns up."

"No," I said. "Thanks, but don't bother. I have had it. If some day Chuck and the others walk in here and give themselves up, I will be glad to come down and sign the necessary papers. Until then, you can keep it."

I went out. I didn't want to go home and I didn't want to go to the office. I didn't particularly want to go anywhere but I couldn't just stand on the corner. I went to Noddy's. After all, it had been more his party than mine. I owed him the explanation.

I gave it to him. He shook his head, his eyes narrow and shrewd, his big hands splayed out on the bar.

"I ain't no cop, but it don't sound right to me. Too much things happening just——" He made a gesture and shrugged.

"Coincidence," I said. "Yeah. But things do happen just that way. I guess I've been doing too much wishful thinking."

"There's a link," said Noddy. "Somewheres. You mark my words."

I marked them and went home. It was almost lunch time now, but I wasn't hungry. I was going to make an excuse and go sour and solitary to my bed, hoping that a sleep might make me fit to be around again.

Tracey and her mother were waiting for me. Tracey looked pale and grim with her banged-up forehead. Mother looked simply and honestly frightened.

"Walt," she said, "you're going to have to do something. I think you should send Tracey and the children to Boston for a while, completely out of reach." She turned to Tracey. "I don't know what your father and I could do to protect you if——"

It was dim and cool and pleasant in the old-fashioned living room. Through the windows I could see the garden blazing with late flowers in the sunshine. I could hear Bets and Pudge playing. I felt suddenly a little faint.

I said, "What happened?"

"We listened to the ten o'clock news," Tracey said nervously. "I don't suppose you heard it?"

"No."

"Well, it told about finding the man's body. It said the police were working on a theory that it was linked with a series of other crimes. It mentioned your name."

"You've simply got to do something," Mother said. "It isn't right."

"Don't worry," I said. "Go on, Tracey."

"The phone rang," she said, and now the fright was becoming audible in her voice, tightening it, tuning it to a raw uncertainty of tone, "about half an hour after the news broadcast. I answered it. I thought it was Mae. She was supposed to be coming to lunch. But it wasn't Mae. It was a man's voice. He asked for you."

Pudge began to bawl furiously. "Mother," said Tracey, "will you quiet him? Please. I'm so nervous I don't know what to do."

Mother went out. I heard her cooing to Pudge, and Tracey went on talking.

"I said you weren't here. It was a pleasant voice, Walt, that's the most dreadful part of it. Pleasant and polite. He said it was a business call and quite important and where could he reach you. I told him—Walt, I'm sorry, but I didn't dream—I told him you were with the police but you'd be back, some time this morning——"

Her voice trailed off. I asked her what he said then.

"It was as much the *way* he said it. His voice got—cruel. He said when you got back to tell you that you'd been warned twice and wouldn't listen, and now you were going to be sorry you'd ever been born. He said the police couldn't help you any more than they ever had. And he hung up."

She looked at me. "It was Chuck, wasn't it?"

"Sounds like him."

"How did he get this number?"

"It wouldn't be hard. One of the gang knew me, he might have told him. Or he could get it from the office if he asked right."

"What are we going to do?"

"Wait a minute. Let me think."

I went over to the window and stared out at the marigolds and the brilliant zinnias. I thought, Boston is a good idea, yes, send them to Boston and I'll go to a hotel, and the folks won't be in any danger then. I thought, The link Noddy was talking about, I know it's there but I can't see it. Chuck wouldn't have called, he wouldn't have threatened me, if Clymer's body meant nothing to him. I was right, I knew I was right, and the link's there if I could only——

Mother's voice, sharp and querulous with fear, and who could blame her? "Walt, you must think of Tracey and the little ones. You——"

"Shut up," I said. "Please. Just a minute. Let me think."

Everett Bush is the link, but he didn't go out that night. He wanted to go out but his parents wouldn't let him.

He wanted to go out.

He wanted to so much there was a fight about it and the old man hit him.

He must have had a definite date, something planned, or he wouldn't have been so insistent.

Something definite, something planned . . .

I went for the phone. "In a minute," I said to Tracey and her mother. "In a minute."

I called Headquarters and asked for Koleski.

I waited a thousand years until he answered.

"I was going out to lunch."

"Lunch, hell. Listen, Pete——"

"I thought you weren't going to bother me any more."

"Something's happened. Will you listen to me? All right." I told him about the phone call. "Doesn't that prove he's mixed up in it? If he's worried enough and scared enough to hunt me out and threaten me about it——"

"I'd say it was a strong indication," said Koleski. His tone had changed. He was interested. "But it's only an indication. It doesn't tie——"

"Call them," I said. "The aunt and uncle. The people you

133

talked to. Ask them if anybody stopped by the house for Everett that night."

He was silent for a minute. Then he said, "I see what you mean. Yeah. Okay, I'll call you back. Oh, and Walt—I'll arrange for a guard."

"Thanks, but I think we'd all feel better if I just get the family out of harm's way for a while."

"Going to let him chase you right out of town?"

"Not me. Women and children only."

"Well, suit yourself, but I'm going to send some men anyway, so Chuck will have company if he does show up."

He rang off. I went back in the living room to talk to Tracey and her mother, and then a car pulled up outside. We were all jumpy as cats, and the sound set us off. Mother screamed, Tracey ran for the kids, and I held up my stick like a club, and it would have been funny as hell except that it wasn't, at least not to us.

Mae walked in with her three young ones.

"Am I late?" she said brightly. "I've been all morning trying to get a sitter for——"

Her voice faded out gradually into nothing. She looked from one to the other of us, and said, "What on earth is the matter?"

"We've been threatened," said Mother.

Tracey began to laugh. "It's only Mae," she said. "Of course." She laughed again and then stopped suddenly and took Mae's little girl and two littler boys out into the garden.

I sat down. "Same old deal," I said. "You startled us, that's all." I explained about the call, and Mae said, "It does seem a damned dirty shame they can't catch those young hoodlums."

"They're going to put a guard on this place," I said. I explained that all over again to Mother. "You'll be perfectly safe."

Mae said, "Why don't you come and stay with us for a while?"

"Thanks," I said, "but you're not using your noodle. If Chuck could find us here he could find us there, and then you'd be in trouble too. No, Tracey and the kids are going up to Boston for a while, out of reach, and I'm going to a hotel. It's me he wants, and if I——"

The phone rang, and again there were white faces and wide eyes. But it was Koleski.

"You were right," he said. "A car did stop by the Bush house that night. They didn't see it but they heard it and heard the driver honk for Everett. Everett went out to explain that he couldn't go. He was awfully sulky about it. He said he'd had a date with 'these guys,' and they'd think he was a baby if he told them his mother wouldn't let him go. Seems the old man got up and said he'd tell 'em himself, and Everett went scuttling out. He wasn't gone more than five minutes."

"You can see what happened," I said. "After all, I hired Finelli to find the gang, not just hold Everett's hand. If he figured this was the car I described, and the boys, he'd follow them whether Everett went with them or not."

"It figures," said Koleski. "I'll see if I can scare up a witness, somebody who actually saw the car and can describe it. Maybe even somebody who saw Finelli. Keep your fingers crossed, kid. And the guard is on the way."

"Thanks, pal," I said, and hung up. I felt better. Much better. Thanks, Chuck, I thought. Thanks for making the phone call. Thanks for being stupid. No, not stupid, really. How were you to know that you were almost in the clear?

All at once Chuck began to seem human and fallible, and not a sort of night demon beyond the reach of mortal hands. I remembered the way he had acted when he threw the stones. He's human, I thought, and he's afraid. He feels us closing in.

And I thought—ominous commonplace—that when a man is frightened is when he's most unpredictable and dangerous. Like any other creature. Like a tiger. Like a rat.

The women had gone out into the kitchen. Mother had a "girl" but apparently it was her day off, because they were getting the lunch themselves. Their voices sounded edgy and shrill and the pots rattled more loudly than usual. I joined them.

"Was it good news?" asked Mae rather sardonically.

"It might be."

"Well, it seems to me," said Mae, "that if you had minded

135

your business and let the police mind theirs in the first place, you wouldn't be in this spot."

I didn't get mad. She was right. "The only trouble with that was that the police had so much more pressing business. And this was sort of personal. Suppose somebody hammered Vince to a pulp?"

"I'd track them down and kill them," said Mae. "I don't blame you. I just think you're crazy." She bustled her three kids into chairs beside Bets and Pudge and helped Tracey make peanut-butter-and-jelly sandwiches for the lot. There was a gooey-looking casserole of some sort in the oven, but the kids knew better than to have anything to do with that. "I can help you pack, Tracey."

"I'm not going anywhere," Tracey said.

"But——"

"That was Walt's idea, not mine. If he's going to get himself killed, I'm not going to be in Boston when it happens." Her voice became loud, strident, almost threatening. "I don't want to hear any more about it, Mother! We'll leave here, that's only right. But I'm not going away."

She turned to Mae. "If we're not there, there wouldn't be any danger. How about letting the children stay with you?"

"But," said Mae, "I——"

"That's silly," I said. "They'd be safer here, under police guard. So would you, if you're set on staying. Oh, hell, we've been over this so many times I'm dizzy. I only know I'm the one he wants, and I'm getting out. So that ought to leave everybody else in the clear."

There was a moment of silence, and then Mae said in a hesitant voice, as though she felt guilty about intruding such a picayune difficulty,

"I will gladly take the kids tomorrow, Tracey, if you want me to, but I'm stuck tonight. Vince has that banquet, and I simply have to go, and at the last minute I can't get a sitter. You certainly won't want to be bothered with my three, so I'll have to arrange to leave them with Mrs. McGrath's sitter, double up——"

I didn't think I could take any more of this. I got up and started toward the door.

Tracey said, "But I thought you had that all fixed up with your Mrs. Liebendorffer. What happened to her?"

"Her boy ran off," said Mae, dealing out the sandwiches, "last Saturday night, and she hasn't heard from him since. She's too hysterical even to answer the phone, poor thing, but her daughter called me."

"I didn't know she had a boy," said Tracey.

"Oh yes. I've only seen him once or twice myself, when he happened to bring her over, but he seemed like a nice boy. Long tall drink of water, about seventeen—her baby, she always called him."

They both turned their heads now and looked at me, because I had come back across the kitchen.

"A tall skinny boy?" I said. "And he ran away last Saturday night?"

Mae put her hand over her mouth, "But he couldn't be the boy you were looking for, Walt."

"What's his name?"

"Adolph," she said. "After Mrs. Liebendorffer's father, I think. I don't see how he could be——"

"Adolph. Not a very happy name for a boy to be saddled with, is it? Does he have a middle name?"

"Now how in the world would I know——" She brought up short, and then said in a small voice, "As a matter of fact, I do know. Mrs. Liebendorffer is a very talkative woman. He has a middle name, for the late Mr. Liebendorffer's father. It's Wilhelm."

Wilhelm. William. Bill. Who in an era cursed with the name of Hitler would not rather be called Bill than Adolph?

"Why did he run away?"

"I don't know. His family doesn't know. He just went."

"When did he go, on Saturday night? Late? Early?"

"For heaven's sake, Walt! Late, I think. He came home late and then in the morning he was gone. At least that's what his sister told me."

"What's the address?"

"Seventeen forty-six North Buckeye. But Walt——"

I didn't wait. As I passed the phone I thought of Koleski, but there was no use trying to call him now. He would be out. Besides, I didn't have any real, definite reason to call, not yet. After I had talked to Mrs. Liebendorffer I would know better.

I got in the car and drove north.

18

NORTH BUCKEYE wasn't as far out as Laurel
Terrace. It was one of those pleasant streets of slightly elderly
frame houses, well kept up and comfortable, shaded by big trees.
I found the number. I parked in front of it and just sat there for
a few minutes, almost afraid to go in and find out whether this
was at last the break, the real honest-to-God break, or only
another blind alley.

Finally I had to get moving. It was a green house with a wide
porch and a neat patch of lawn with hydrangeas in a row against
the wall. I climbed the steps. They were wooden, painted that
season. They rang hollow under my feet. I crossed the porch
and rang the bell.

A woman answered it, so quickly that I thought she must have
been peering out at my car and wondering what I was doing. She
was a young woman with a distracted, angry face. Yet there was
something eager about the way she asked me what I wanted.

I told her who I was, and eagerness was replaced by disappointment. She said rather snappishly, "I called your sister
and explained why my mother couldn't come tonight. I'm sorry
if she's been inconvenienced——"

"It isn't that," I said. "I want to talk to Mrs. Liebendorffer
about the boy."

Now the eagerness came back again. "About Adolph? Do you
know something?"

"I'm not sure. That's why I want to talk to Mrs.
Liebendorffer."

From somewhere inside a voice cried, "Who is it, Marthe? Is
it news?"

"I don't know, Mother," she answered. "It's Mr. Sherris, and he wants to see you." She stepped aside for me to come past her. Lowering her voice, she said savagely, "Do you know where he is? If I ever get my hands on that young whelp——"

She looked as though she had had a rough four days.

A hall ran along this side of the house, with the doors opening off to the right. In the nearest doorway a woman stood, holding a wrapper around her with one hand and clinging with the other to the jamb, as though she was too weak to stand unaided. It was a minute before I recognized her. I had been introduced to Mrs. Liebendorffer at Mae's house, and I remembered her as a neat, placid, pleasant soul. Now her gray hair hung in wild straggles, her eyes were sunk into dark holes behind her rimless glasses, her plump pink cheeks had lost their color and their firmness.

"Sherris?" she said. "Sherris? I don't—— Oh yes, Mrs. Farrel's brother. Mr. Sherris, I can't possibly come tonight, I've has a terrible shock and I'm simply not able. I should think your sister would understand that, being a mother herself."

I explained all over again that I was not trying to get her to baby-sit. "I want to talk to you about Bill."

She stared at me blankly. "Bill?"

"About Adolph, Mother," said Marthe. To me she said, "Everybody else calls him Bill, but Mother sticks to Adolph. Shall we go in and sit down?"

"It's a good name," said Mrs. Liebendorffer, wiping her eyes. "It was my father's name. One bad man should not spoil a good name." She allowed herself to be led to a couch and placed in a rumpled nest of pillows and eider down. "Please—what do you know about my Adolph?"

"Perhaps nothing," I said. "It might have been some other boy. Do you happen to know where he went Saturday night— before he ran away, I mean?"

"To a movie," said Mrs. Liebendorffer. "Adolph is a good boy. He always told me where he was going, until now. I can't understand why he would do this. I'd have understood, no matter how much trouble he's in."

"You're sure he's in trouble? I mean, boys do sometimes get the urge to go out on their own."

"Oh, no. He left a note." She searched for it through the folds of her clothing and handed me a crumpled piece of paper. "You can see he's frightened out of his wits, poor child. If he'd only talked to me first——"

I read the note. *I got to go away for a while, Mom, I am in trouble. DON'T have the police look for me unless you want to see me in jail. I will come back when it's safe. Don't worry, Mom, I love you.*

There was no signature. I suppose there hadn't really been any need for one.

I said, "And you haven't notified the police that he was missing?"

She shook her head. "I kept thinking surely he would come back. Every day, every night—I've been out of my head with worry, Mr. Sherris, but it seemed he would have to come back soon, because he didn't have much money."

"He took all there was in the house," Marthe said. "About twenty dollars." She made an impatient gesture. "It isn't as though he'd been kidnapped or was in any danger. He's bound to come home when he gets hungry enough, and trust to Mother to fight his battles for him. After all, he's not the first boy to run away because he's got some girl in trouble."

"Marthe, Marthe," whispered Mrs. Liebendorffer. "And in front of a stranger."

Feeling the beginnings of despair, I said, "A girl? He doesn't say anything in the note about a girl."

"Of course not. *He* was quiet as a clam. But Chuck told us."

Just like that.

Chuck told us.

I sat there, in that stuffy comfortable room with the flowered slip covers and the mantel loaded with family photographs, and watched the piece of paper I held in my hand blur out of sight into a strange darkness. And somewhere in the darkness a woman said, *Chuck told us.*

I said, speaking carefully as though too loud a tone would frighten the word away, "Chuck?"

"A friend of Adolph's," said Marthe impatiently. Obviously

Chuck was of no importance to her. "He came over Sunday because of the camping trip, and when he found out Adolph was gone he said that must be the reason."

"He did," I said. "Yes, he would, of course. That would be the right thing to say. But he didn't tell you the girl's name, did he?"

"No, he said he didn't know who she was, only that Bill— Adolph—was mixed up with her. What do you mean, it would be the right thing to say? What are you talking about, Mr. Sherris?"

Her voice sounded a little queer and edgy. I could see my hands again. They were still holding the note but they were shaking so I couldn't make out the words. I tried to get them out of sight until they quieted.

I asked, "What is Chuck's last name?"

"It's Landry. Why?"

"He's a big boy, isn't he? Eighteen years old, tall, good-looking?"

"A nice boy," said Mrs. Liebendorffer. "Very well-spoken and polite." She had forgotten to cry for the moment. She was looking at me with the faint beginning of alarm.

"That is what he looks like, though?"

"Yes," said Marthe, "but I don't see what difference——"

"There are three other boys too. They travel together, the five of them. Bill, and Chuck, and a short stocky boy with a loud laugh——"

"Roy Aspinwall," she said, and now her voice was very quiet.

"And Everett Bush," I said, and she nodded. "And one other."

"Bobby Stillman. Yes. They've been friends for quite a while. But how do you know them?"

"In a minute," I said. "Just a minute." I sat in the chair with every nerve aching and the names banging in my ears like drums. Bush. Aspinwall. Stillman.

And Landry.

No more attacks from ambush, no more happy violence, no more hunting in the night. No more fun for any of you.

Now you have names.

Now I will find you and drag you out into the light.

That's what I thought. It was a good thought. There was only one thing the matter with it. It wasn't so.

Marthe was talking to me. She wanted to know how I knew these boys and why I was so curious about her brother. I shook my head.

"If you knew how long I've waited," I said. "I'm sorry. Listen, did your Bill go with them Saturday night?"

"Yes," said Mrs. Liebendorffer. "They often went to the movies together."

"But Everett wasn't with them."

"They just stopped outside and honked," said Marthe. "I don't know who was in the car."

"A light-colored convertible," I said.

"Sort of a gray-blue. It belongs to Chuck."

"Nice boy," said Mrs. Liebendorffer. "Adolph never went with rowdies." Her gaze had been drawn to my bad leg, and she was staring at it as though it had a horrible fascination for her.

"My sister must have told you what happened to me," I said. "About four months ago. Remember?"

She formed a word with her mouth, but nothing came for a long minute. Then she said loudly, emphatically, "No. Not Adolph. Not my son. He was not one of the boys who beat you."

"Your son didn't touch me," I said. "And I doubt very much if he's ever touched anybody else, either. But he's been running with a bad bunch and he's in bad trouble, and it doesn't have anything to do with a girl."

She looked at me with great suffering eyes. Marthe now had moved over to stand protectively beside her. I felt like a barbarian with a club, poised to strike them.

"The boys didn't go to the movies," I said. "They went a lot farther than that. Two men were killed Saturday night, and I think your Bill was a witness. And I think he ran away in fear of his own life."

The silence in the room was not long but it was heavy. You could feel the weight of it.

Then Marthe said, "You're making a terrible accusation."

"He's crazy," said Mrs. Liebendorffer suddenly, in a cracked, wild voice. "My boy went to the movies Saturday night. My boy is a good boy. He never hurt anyone." She got to her feet, screeching at me. "Get out, you crazy man. Get out, get out!"

She fell back on the couch, sobbing.

I wouldn't have believed that this moment—the time when I had actually got the names of the boys and would shortly have their addresses—could be so distasteful and unjoyous to me.

I looked at Marthe. "Please try to understand. I haven't anything against your brother. He could have saved me a lot if he'd gone for the police but he was evidently afraid to, and since I've come to know Chuck better I don't blame him. It's very important to find him, both as a witness against the others, and for his own safety. If the boys find him first, they'll surely kill him now."

I don't know how much of that she heard. She was thinking of something else.

"That was about the time," she said. "Four months ago."

"What?"

"He began acting queer, as though there was something on his mind. I remember a couple of times he said he was sick and had me tell the boys he couldn't go out with them. And then once we found him in his room all doubled up with pain with big bruises on his stomach. He said he got hurt playing tag football."

I remembered what the can-ganger, Suby, had said—how four of the boys were hustling and roughing the fifth one, threatening him in an only partly jesting way.

"I think they've been afraid from the first that he'd tell on them," I said. "He didn't really belong. They got him involved right up to his neck so he wouldn't dare to turn against them, but I guess Saturday was too much for him."

It would have been too much for most boys, I thought. That nightmarish business in the strip mine, the mounting terror, and then the discovery that they had been seen and the killing of Finelli. Bill must have come home sick and surfeited with death, caught between an overpowering sense of guilt and fear for his own safety. And he had done the only thing he could think of to do. He had started running, blindly, to escape the day of reckoning.

Something Marthe had said recurred to me. "What was that about a camping trip? Was Bill supposed to go away with the boys?"

"Monday," said Marthe slowly, still looking dazed. "To Cook's Forest."

"How nice," I said. "How normal and healthy. But Bill was too smart to go with them. You can be thankful for that."

He must have pictured himself in the vast dim solitudes under the primeval trees, alone with Chuck and Roy and Bobby, those quiet well-spoken boys. He must have thought of all the innocent-seeming, apparently accidental ways in which his tongue and his conscience might have been permanently removed as a threat to his companions. No wonder he had run away.

And Chuck must have sweated a bloody sweat of fear ever since Sunday morning, wondering whether Bill would give himself up and talk.

Now I understood Chuck's wild tantrum when he failed to kill me, and I understood his phone call of this morning. He was scared. Things were slipping away from him, out of his control. He had to do something, anything, and he was already in so deep that he had very little to lose and much to gain if he could get me, his worst enemy, off his trail, or get a dangerous witness out of the way. Or both. Preferably both.

"Do you have any idea at all where Bill could have gone?"

Marthe answered. Mrs. Liebendorffer seemed beyond speech. "We've done everything we could think of to find him. Called all our relatives, all our friends, all the places he used to go around—you know, malt shops, places like that. There isn't a trace of him."

She sat down, white-faced, her hands caught together in her lap. "I just can't take all this in," she said. "It's too——" She shook her head, unable to find any word that would fit.

"I know," I said.

"Isn't there a chance you could be wrong?"

"Do you think it's likely?"

"No. You knew the boys. But——" Her mind was turning this way and that, searching desperately for hope. "Even if they are the boys who beat you, are you sure they did these—these other horrible things?"

"I think so. The police think so too. But Bill can tell us. For sure." I got up. "Has Chuck been around again or called since Sunday?"

"No. He's gone. He and Roy and Bobby went ahead on their camping trip anyway, without my brother."

"The hell they did," I said. "I saw Chuck Monday afternoon. He hurt my wife and came within an ace of killing both of us. He made a threatening phone call no more than two hours ago. He's right here in Mall's Ford."

She thought about that for a moment. "I don't understand how that could be. I called their homes, all of them, hoping they might have heard from Adolph. Their parents said they hadn't, and the boys were still gone."

This was bad. It meant that the boys had lied to their parents. It meant that they were free of all supervision and all annoyances of routine, able to put their whole strength into doing whatever they might feel was necessary to protect themselves. It meant that picking them up was not going to be as simple as I had thought.

"How long were they supposed to be gone?"

"A week. They were to come back next Sunday night."

Then their parents would not expect to hear from them until then. The boys would have a clear field, as long as they kept out of sight.

My young tigers were still at large.

I picked up the phone and called Koleski.

19

Aɴᴅ ᴛʜᴀᴛ was my Big Break, the cap and crown of more than four months' labor. By afternoon of the next day, Thursday, we were in possession of the following information:

Chuck Landry, Roy Aspinwall, and Bobby Stillman had left their homes very early on Monday morning. Their parents believed that they had gone to Cook's Forest to camp out.

The park administration at Cook's Forest had no record of any camping permit being issued in any of these three names, nor were the boys in any of the local motels or cabins.

Everett Bush was still in Cincinnati.

Adolph Wilhelm Liebendorffer was still missing.

There was a little more. Koleski and Hartigan now had Chuck's license number and a description of the car. But they had not been able to turn up a single witness who had seen Finelli's car near the Bush place on Saturday night, nor any witness who had seen Finelli following Chuck's car, there or anywhere. Neither had they been able to place the four boys near the strip mine.

The Big Break was something less than a blazing success.

Koleski and Hartigan came over to the Ohio Hotel to tell me what the score was. I had moved myself and my family in yesterday afternoon, much to my mother-in-law's relief, and it did not seem possible that anyone could get to Tracey and the children there. The management and the hotel detective had been alerted so that we were in effect under twenty-four-hour guard. I had not gone to work, on Koleski's suggestion. He felt that I ought to avoid all familiar or routine actions—just in case.

"It won't be very long now," he said. "We've got names, we know who we're looking for, and we have one big advantage. They don't know we're onto them."

"Yes," I said, "but how long is long enough? Suppose Bill falls under a bus or something. Suppose——"

"Suppose you let us do the best we can. Look, Walt, you've done all right. Now relax. We have an all-points bulletin out. All the surrounding cities have been notified, Cleveland, Akron, Pittsburgh, and especially Newbridge and the Pennsylvania border towns. Somewhere the Liebendorffer boy will show, and we'll get him. So will the others. It's only a matter of a little time."

"Yes," I said. "Sure. I know."

"Their parents must feel terrible," Tracey said, holding Pudge a little tighter in her lap. Bets was having a terrific affair with Hartigan. Koleski sighed.

"I don't think they believe it yet," he said. "That's nearly always the worst of it in cases like this—the relatives, the wives and husbands and parents who just can't believe that the person in question could possibly commit a crime."

"I'm sorry for them," Tracey said. "What kind of people are they?"

I had not seen any of them, of course, and I was glad. Mrs. Liebendorffer had been enough.

"Nice people," said Koleski. "Civilized. Plenty of money, but not too much. Good homes. The psychiatrists may be able to figure out some reason why the boys turned out the way they did, but there's nothing showing on the surface. With the Bush boy, now——"

"He's lucky," I said. "He should be damned thankful that he wasn't allowed to go out that night."

"It's a pity any of them ever got together," Hartigan said over his shoulder. Bets was doing her best to steal his nice shiny badge that she had wheedled him into showing her. "One by one they might never have got into any worse trouble than a lot of boys get into and outgrow."

The five, it turned out, went to different schools, which was why Davenport had not been able to get far with Northside High.

The Liebendorffer boy went there, like Everett, ʳ ᵔ ᵒy Aspin-wall and Bobby Stillman went to private schools and Chuck Landry was in college. The meeting ground seemed to have been a record shop on the north side, specializing in the kind of music kids like. A perfectly innocent place, with a pizza palace and a hobby shop next door. No wickedness had been provided for them there. The boys hadn't needed it, anyway. They had brought their own.

Koleski said, "They must have discovered they were soul mates and started to go around together, and sooner or later some spark was bound to set them off. It was your tough luck, Walt, that you had to be around when it happened."

"Yeah. Well," I said, "it's all over now but the waiting. I just hope Bill has sense enough to keep out of their way."

"Now, how," said Koleski reasonably, "can they find him so easily, if we can't?"

It was a good question. It was eminently sensible. The only comeback I had for it was that nothing in this whole thrice-damned business had gone the way it should have.

And all I could think of was Bill Liebendorffer, the donkey who had tried running with the tigers and who now was running away from them, alone and afraid and so pitifully young.

"Let's see those pictures again," I said.

Koleski gave them to me. The one of Chuck Landry was a handsome portrait of a handsome young man. The one of Bobby Stillman was a handsome portrait of an unhandsome but totally undistinguished young man. The one of Roy Aspinwall was a snapshot of a boy grinning and squinting in the sun. They didn't mean anything to me. They were just pictures. They did not in any way reflect the living realities that I knew so intimately. Perhaps this was how they looked by day, and their personalities, vampire-fashion, came out only after dark.

I shook my head and gave them back to Koleski, keeping the one of Adolph Wilhelm Liebendorffer a minute longer. This too was a snapshot, rather fuzzy, of a tall thin boy with a narrow face, standing in front of the house on North Buckeye.

He had long legs. I hoped he knew how to use them.

The phone rang while Koleski was restoring all the photos to their envelope. It was for him, from Headquarters. He listened for a minute, and then he said, in his professional voice, "Right, we're on our way."

Hartigan set my daughter gently on her feet and stood up.

"Holdup," said Koleski, setting the phone down. "Gas station on Logan Road. They shot the guy." He was halfway out the door when he paused long enough to say, "Keep out of trouble, Walt. I am liable to be too busy to help."

He nodded to Tracey and was gone.

Tracey asked, "Who got shot?"

"I'm not sure," I said. "Probably the station attendant."

Tracey looked at the sunlit window and shivered. "And I used to think the world was such a friendly place."

I patted her shoulder. "Well," I said, "as far as we're concerned, Pete's right. All we have to do now is wait."

We waited.

It wasn't so bad. The kids thought hotel life was delightful, eating in unfamiliar places, riding the elevator, pestering a practically endless supply of people. Tracey finally got them to bed long after their usual hour, and I sat with her, talking, until she turned in. I was too restless even to try. I went downstairs and bought a late paper and sat in the bar reading it and envying all the people who could freely walk in and out and around the streets at will, unafraid.

I thought of Adolph Wilhelm Liebendorffer, who was walking the streets somewhere out there in the night, starting at every sound, fleeing from every shadow, not knowing what to do or where to go.

He's had five days, I thought. Five days to sweat and tremble, fighting it out with his conscience. He knows what he ought to do. He knows what he's got to do to save himself, to save others. He can't go on much longer, no matter how scared he is. He's bound to crack. He's bound to give himself up.

Or is he? It's a wide world. Why doesn't he just get lost in it?

I ordered another beer and read the paper gloomily.

There was a story on the gas-station holdup. Two men described as being in their early twenties had shoved guns at the attendant and demanded his cash. They had become alarmed and one of them had shot the attendant. They had cleaned out the till, netting thirty-two dollars and forty-nine cents. The major part of the station's receipts had already been taken to the bank. The robbers had got away. The attendant, an army veteran with a wife and child, was on the critical list.

Crime. You read about it every day.

There is a legend in this land that major crimes are cleverly planned by clever crooks or clever murderers who stand to gain a fortune. Once in a while they are. Once in a while somebody knocks over Brink's for a million or two, and once in a while some woman collects a tidy packet in insurance for each one of a long line of husbands. But most crimes are just plain stupid, stupidly done by stupid people. Joe Nameless is insanely jealous of his sloppy wife. Some fool has got a high-school girl in trouble. A couple of morons decide to make a fortune holding up a gas station. Kids mug old ladies for the pennies in their purses. Stupid. You wish to heaven criminals did have brains. You'd feel so much safer.

A young man liable to die for the sake of thirty-two dollars, and think of his wife and what she's going through. Me and my family hiding in a hole, our lives totally disrupted and made hideous, for nothing. Mrs. Liebendorffer, out of her senses with worry and shame. Three sets of parents just becoming aware that the world has changed for them today and will never be quite the same again. All for nothing. Multiply us by hundreds, thousands. Add the parents of the little girl who went to the corner store for a bottle of milk and never came back, or the little boy found strangled in a wood, or the housewife murdered by a total stranger. Count the names and the misery. Number the victims of the tiger, the careless blood-hungry tiger that is always in our midst. The goddamned stupid tiger.

It dawned on me that I was one of the luckiest victims.

I felt sick and depressed. I went upstairs and went to bed.

I lay for a long time in that dim shadowy state that isn't quite awake or quite asleep, where the thoughts you have been thinking often take a queer turn, and things are illumined by a clear gray light, oblique and colorless but strangely bright.

I thought about Bill Liebendorffer on the run. I saw him on a dark street. No particular street, just a composite image of old brick fronts that could have been anywhere. At the same time I thought of what had happened to me that night on Williams Avenue, and how Bill had hung back, and how he had run to the car and crouched there, taking no part in what was going on.

There was a connection there. I didn't try to figure it out. I just let it come.

After a while it did. I could testify that Bill had taken no part. That would go far to help persuade the police that Bill had had no part in the other things that happened either, but had been forced to go along under threat of injury so that he wouldn't dare to tell on his pals. I could be a friend to Bill or I could be a bitter enemy, and it would make a great deal of difference. Bill might want to know, before he made up his mind to take the plunge, just how I felt about him.

I could go even farther than that. I could imagine that Bill might feel that unless he could get me on his side—the original victim saying, *This boy was innocent*—it would be hopeless to try and make anyone believe that he wasn't as guilty as Chuck.

I could picture Bill thinking, *If Sherris backs me up I'll tell the police all about it, but if he doesn't I'll run far away and hope never to be heard of again.*

And in this dopey half-world I was in I could see Bill writing notes and making calls on telephones, but the notes lay unread in a big white rural mailbox marked SHERRIS, and the telephone rang and rang in an empty house.

The fantasy stayed with me until I did, finally, go to sleep. By the time I woke up again it had receded and grown faint, remaining as a kind of uneasy prodding at the back of my mind.

Maybe I would have forgotten it completely if anything new had turned up. But it was one of those obstinately blank days when you are wild to hear something, but everyone you know has entered into a conspiracy of silence. I fidgeted around the room, barely able to stand my own wife and children. I called the Liebendorffer home, but Marthe had not heard anything either. I called Koleski, but he was out. The desk sergeant, or whoever it was I talked to, seemed to think he would be out indefinitely.

Hartigan, too. I managed to get hold of Davenport in Juvenile, but he didn't have anything to say either.

"For heaven's sake," said Tracey, "stop pacing up and down like that. You're driving me crazy."

"Sorry," I said. I sat down. Then I got up again.

"What now?" asked Tracey. She looked at me and then she rose and put her arms around me. "Be patient, Walt. You found out who they are, you did what you wanted to do. Be patient now. Don't give them any chance at you."

"No," I said. "Of course I won't."

"You're worrying about that boy, aren't you?"

I had to admit I was.

With just a trace of hardness in her voice, Tracey said, "He got himself into this, you didn't."

"I know," I said, thinking of Mrs. Liebendorffer, "but he's our witness, Tracey. If anything happens to him or he can't be found, we don't have much of a case."

"You can certainly swear to what they did to you."

"And I know what a really good defense attorney could do to me in court, too. On my identification, I mean."

I was still thinking of Mrs. Liebendorffer. The state and I would both lose if anything happened to Bill. But we wouldn't lose anything like as much as Mrs. Liebendorffer.

"Well," said Tracey, "I don't see what you can do about it, anyway."

I didn't myself.

"I think I'll go over to the garage and see how the car's coming," I said. I had taken it in to have the damaged glass replaced. "Now for Pete's sake, Tracey—it's broad daylight and I'll take a cab. Let's not carry this to where it's ridiculous."

She smothered the quick look of alarm that had come into her eyes. "All right, Walt," she said, and sat down again. I realized how badly Chuck's phone call had frightened her. I bent and kissed her. "Don't worry, honey," I said, and went out, knowing that of course she would worry until I came in again.

I couldn't help it. I couldn't sit in that hotel room any longer.

I took a cab to the garage. The car was ready and I drove it out into the sunlit streets. I wanted to go out to the house. If Bill had tried, or was trying, to get in touch with me, that would be where he would do it. He would probably not have any way of knowing that I wasn't staying there.

But Chuck knew. He had called my father-in-law's house when he wanted to threaten me. He would not be looking for me at the other place at all.

Probably the safest place in town for me, I thought. But I went the long way around, swinging westward and then back to come onto Laurel Terrace from the north, avoiding the north road and the glen where Chuck had ambushed us. I did not see anything of a gray convertible, anywhere along the line, and the street was peaceful in the late summer warmth. Children played, dogs barked, women worked in flower beds or hung up clothes, and certainly violence would never touch this well-fed community.

I parked in front of the house I owned but was afraid to live in.

Andy White's wife, Jane, spotted me from where she was cutting flowers in her garden, and came to meet me, asking how we all were. I talked to her while I got the mail out of the box at the curb. There was quite an accumulation of paper there. I riffled through it. Nothing.

I thought, well, so much for that, and tossed the mail into the car. A boy about twelve years old rode by on a bicycle. He had a small brown-and-white dog with him. He and the dog lived three houses up and across the street. He looked at me intently, and the dog woofed. Jane waved to the boy and I nodded, and he waved back and then went pedaling furiously down the street, with the dog after him.

"Has anybody been around?" I asked Jane.

"Not a soul," she said, and then went on to elaborate. Finally I said I had to go, and she told me to give her love to Tracey and the little ones and she certainly did miss us. "Oh, and, Walt, would you want us to do anything about phone calls?"

"How do you mean?" I asked, every nerve springing to attention.

"Well, we were out in the yard last night, it was so warm, and we could hear the phone ringing and ringing in your place. We were afraid it might be important but of course we couldn't get in, and I was going to say that if you wanted to leave us a key I'd be glad——"

And there it was, the telephone that rang in an empty house. I had guessed right.

Then I caught myself. It still didn't have to be Bill calling. Everyone else who would have any reason to call me knew I wasn't there, but it still didn't have to be Bill. It could be someone I hardly knew. It could be an insurance salesman or a telephone canvasser. It could be a wrong number.

"No," I said slowly, "if that's the call I hope it is, nobody could take it but me."

"Something about the case?" she asked eagerly.

"Yes. I don't know. Maybe."

If he had called last night, and no one had answered, would he try again? Or had I missed my chance? Had I got my bright idea too late?

"What time was that?" I asked.

"Around ten. Maybe a little earlier. If it was really important, they'll call again. Listen," she said, "we'll be home. Why don't you wait with us? We can sit out in the garden where you can hear the phone if it rings, and Andy can keep an eye on the house."

"Thanks," I said, "but I guess I'll just go in now and stick right beside the phone."

That was the beginning of a long afternoon, and an even longer night.

20

I CALLED Tracey, of course, first thing, to let her know where I was. She was not happy about it, but after some fairly heated words I managed to convince her that I was going to stay there.

"I can't take a chance on missing him again," I said.

"If he calls again, and if it was Bill. It seems to me that you've dreamed this one up right out of your own head, just because you can't stand it not to be doing something."

I agreed with her that it was perfectly possible. Even probable. Just the same, I was going to stay.

"Well, I'm going to let Mr. Koleski know about it."

I told her to go ahead, not adding that Mr. Koleski had other things to do at the moment beside worry about where I was.

"Anyway, honey, this is the last place the boys would expect to find me." I explained that all over again carefully. "And I won't take any chances."

She did not argue it any further. "When will you call me?"

"As soon as I know. It might be late, really late. So don't worry." Don't worry, indeed. I wondered how many thousands of times I had said those meaningless words already.

I said good-by, and then settled myself in the most comfortable chair near the telephone. I had put the car in the garage and closed the doors, so that no casual passer-by could tell that it was there. When night came I would not put on any lights. I had my gun. All I had to do was sit.

I could see a thin segment of street between the window curtains. The boy on the bicycle rode by going the other way, with the brown-and-white dog bounding behind him. After that there was nothing but an occasional car.

The afternoon wore on. Nothing happened. The house was warm and stuffy. I got heavy-headed but I didn't want to sleep. I got hungry and found a box of cookies in the kitchen, and washed them down with tap water. They were very sweet cookies, and I did not feel well after I ate them. My leg took a spell of aching, and no matter how I squirmed and twisted I couldn't ease it. I was bored to the point of madness and too petulant to read.

And the damned phone would not ring.

It was not going to ring. The whole thing was a pipe dream, and Bill was a thousand miles away by now.

Or it would ring, and it would turn out to be good old So-and-So you used to know in the Army, in town for a few days, and how are you?

The shadows got longer and deeper and the light went out of the sky.

Someone knocked.

I nearly came out of my skin, but it was only Andy and Jane, bringing sandwiches and a Thermos of coffee. I was starved again and grateful, and I said so. We sat around in the dark for a while, talking, and they tried to get me to come and sit in their yard, but I didn't want to run the risk of not being able to get back in time if the phone did ring. It was kind of creepy in the house with all the lights out. I didn't blame them for wanting to go. I asked Jane to call Tracey for me, and she said she would. It was lonesome after they left. The Thompsons, on the other side, were out.

And the phone sat on its table as dead and cold and disinterested as though it had never rung in its life.

I went to sleep.

I had no intention of doing it and I don't know when it happened. But I must have slept, because all of a sudden I woke up with a wild yell, jumping halfway out of my chair, in a lather of sweat.

And the phone was ringing.

I answered it. An operator said she had a call from Newbridge,

Pennsylvania, for a Mr. Walter Sherris. I said I was speaking, and she told her party to go ahead.

For a minute there was nothing but the hum of an open line, and a sound as of someone breathing a long way off. Then there was a voice.

"Do you still want to know who beat you up?" it said. It was a young, uncertain voice. It had fear in it, so much fear that I was almost afraid to answer, lest I scare it away.

"Yes," I said. "I do."

"There was one of the gang that never touched you, Mr. Sherris, remember? Remember, Mr. Sherris?"

"I remember."

"That was me. I never wanted to hurt anybody. Listen, I can tell you a lot of things if you'll help me. I need help, Mr. Sherris."

He sounded as though he did. "I'll help you," I said. "I haven't anything against you."

"That isn't what Chuck said. He said I was just as guilty as the rest, and you'd put me right in jail with them."

"Chuck was wrong," I said. Sweat was running down my back and my heart was hammering. Please God, I thought, let me not say the wrong thing and queer it.

The voice spoke in my ear, strained, quivering, with an underlying note of hysteria all ready to break.

"You might just be saying that to get hold of me. I want to talk to you. But I got to be sure. I don't want to hang, Mr. Sherris. I'm not guilty of any of it, and I don't want to hang."

Now he was crying. Not exactly like a child and not like a man, either. It was a pitiful sound.

"What shall I do," I asked, "to show you I mean what I say?"

He got his voice steadied again, with an effort.

"You be on the Diamond here in Newbridge at ten-thirty. Walk around. That's all. Walk around. If you're all alone, no cops with you, nobody, then I'll talk to you. I got to be sure, Mr. Sherris. Please don't try anything."

That *please* got me.

"I won't," I said. "But I'll give you a tip. Chuck's out for blood. He tried to kill me Monday afternoon and he threatened me again yesterday, and you know what he'll do to you if he finds you. So be careful. Real careful."

I didn't mention that the police were also looking for him. I didn't dare.

"Why do you think I'm doing this?" he whimpered. "Sometimes I think I'd rather hang than have him and Roy after me. Wear something so I'll know you."

"That's easy," I said. "A brace on my left leg, and a cane. You'll know me. Ten-thirty, on the Newbridge Diamond."

He was gone.

And now I had a choice. I could call the police and ask them to arrange with the Newbridge police to stake out the Diamond and try to catch Bill when he came. And maybe they would catch him and maybe they wouldn't. Maybe he would take fright and run away for good, feeling that I had betrayed him and it was no use. Maybe there would be one of those unhappy accidents that do occur, and Bill would get himself shot, and that would be a lovely thing to remember for the rest of my life.

Or I could go quietly over to Newbridge and meet Bill the way he wanted it.

I could see several reasons for doing it that way. I wanted him to co-operate, and he wouldn't if he was afraid. I wanted to keep him out of trouble. And I wanted him to give himself up voluntarily. It would look a lot better than an arrest.

I couldn't see any reason for not doing it his way except a consideration for my own safety, but I certainly was not afraid of Bill, and I didn't see how I would be in any more danger on the Diamond in Newbridge than I was anywhere else. Unless Chuck had a crystal ball in good working order, there was no way he could know I was going there. At least I couldn't think of any.

I picked up the phone and dialed White's number. Andy answered.

"Listen, Andy," I said, "I got my call. After I'm gone, will you call Tracey and tell her that, and tell her I'm liable to be very late indeed, but everything's working out fine."

"She'll want to know where you're going."

"And you don't know, because I'm not telling you. I'm afraid

Tracey would yell for the police and spoil everything. That's why you're calling her instead of me. Okay? I'm going now."

"Okay," said Andy dubiously. "I'll watch you out."

There was no sight or sound of anything suspicious. I went out of Laurel Terrace Drive the way I came, the long way round. I had plenty of time. The night was cloudy, and the neighborhood too splendidly suburban for adequate street lighting. If there was any car following me, it was too far back to be seen. There were no headlights, anyway.

I angled over to a north-south through route and came down onto 422, the Newbridge road, east of town but not far enough east to suit me. I passed the curve where Finelli was killed. I passed the strip mine were Artie Clymer had died. An ill-omened road, I thought, and wished that I had picked some other way to go.

There were headlights behind me now, but that was natural. 422 is a public highway, and people do use it.

I kept reassuring myself that there was no logical way in which Chuck could have caught up with me. He would not waste his precious days keeping watch over an empty house. He could not afford to. And it was asking too much of coincidence that he should have accidentally happened to see me go by somewhere. I had come to have an almost superstitious fear of the boys. It was understandable, but foolish.

Nevertheless, I kept an eye on the rearview mirror.

I did not see anything alarming. Just headlights. Occasionally a pair would catch up to me and then go by, and every time this happened I got nervous pangs in the belly. I couldn't help it, and it made me angry. It's because I'm so close to the end, I thought. In fifteen or twenty minutes I'll meet Bill and we'll have him safe. There isn't a thing to worry about. This is merely the irrational fear you get, say, when you have decided to take out an insurance policy and are suddenly certain that you will get hit by a truck or struck by lightning before the papers are signed.

I drove on down the dark road, and the headlights, the innocent headlights, came behind me.

I got into Newbridge well before ten-thirty and parked on the

Diamond in front of the post office. Mall's Ford has a square with a Civil War monument in it consisting of a pillar inscribed with the names of battles, and topped by the iron figure of a soldier. Newbridge has a diamond with a Civil War monument in it. Newbridge is smaller than Mall's Ford and less heavily industrial. Newbridge is in Pennsylvania and Mall's Ford is in Ohio. Otherwise there is not much difference.

I looked carefully around but I could not see anything except the normal traffic and the normal number of people on the sidewalk. I got out of the car and began to walk slowly around the Diamond.

By the third or fourth time I had made the circuit I was beginning to feel silly and conspicuous. I had studied the window displays in the gents' clothing store, the furniture store, the appliance store, and the credit jeweler's, until I was afraid I would get picked up for loitering.

I was also getting worried. There was no sign of a tall thin frightened boy who wanted to talk to me.

I went round again, past the hotel, the corner tavern, the dairy store, the Congregational church, the newsstand where they would shine your shoes and block your hat, the post office, and back to the hotel. Four or five men standing in front of the tavern looked at me as I passed, obviously wondering what the hell I was up to. There was an alley beside the hotel. I crossed it slowly, having about made up my mind to go back to the tavern and let Bill find me there if he wanted me.

Then somebody spoke to me.

I turned and looked down the alley, narrow between its walls of brick, the rough sunken pavement holding a greasy glimmer from the light that leaked in from the streets at both ends. There were doorways in the brick walls, closed, showing as arches of blacker shadow, like niches in an abandoned church.

Someone was standing in one of those niches, speaking my name.

21

I TURNED and walked down the alley. The dim figure remained huddled in its niche, waiting, I suppose, to make sure no one came into the alley after me.

No one did, and after a minute the figure ventured out to join me. It was tall and skinny, with a kind of furtive stoop to the narrow shoulders.

"Mr. Sherris," it said.

"Yes," I said. "Hello, Bill."

The light from the corner struck tentatively on his face. His eyes were wide and stary, with dark smudges around them. His features were thin and masculine, but they were his mother's features even so. Perhaps the resemblance was stronger than usual because of the state of emotion they were both in. It was not in any way a bad face. Very young even for its age, not too blazingly brilliant, and reflecting no great strength of character, the face of the sheep and not of the shepherd, but not bad. He caught his breath in between his teeth and started to speak and then didn't. It seemed that now he had me he didn't know what to do with me.

"I'm all alone," I said, "and I meant what I told you. This isn't a very good place to talk; where can we go?"

I was in a fidget lest the cop on the beat should see us and get curious. Bill looked nervously up and down the alley. People went by on the streets at both ends, but otherwise nothing moved.

"Let's just walk around," he said. "Can't we do that?"

He was still afraid of a trap. And he was plain afraid, period.

You could hardly expect him, under the circumstances, to make perfect sense. Seventeen is a poor age for a moment of decision upon which your whole future depends.

"Let's walk out of here, anyway," I said. "We'll attract too much attention hanging around in alleys. Go ahead, you lead."

He began to walk away from the Diamond toward the far end of the alley. He was wearing blue jeans and a jacket, both very dirty and rumpled. The pockets of the jacket bulged, probably with what belongings he had brought with him. He looked as though he had been sleeping in barns and ditches.

On impulse, I said, "Are you hungry?"

He hesitated and then admitted that he was. "I been saving my money. I haven't got much and I thought I might need it."

"You pick the place," I said. "I'll buy. And that's better than trying to talk in the street."

Once more he glanced around, but there was no sign of pursuit. "There's a lunchroom around the corner," he said. "They stay open late."

We went to the lunchroom. It was one of those long narrow holes with a counter at one side and a cramped row of booths along the other. It smelled horribly of stale grease, but it was Bill's stomach, not mine. There were very few customers. We sat down in one of the booths and I ordered coffee and told the counterman to bring Bill anything he wanted.

He wanted hamburgers, and while they were being made we sat in uneasy silence, he staring covertly at my face and keeping his own averted, shy and stricken in the hard glare of the light. He had insisted on sitting where he could watch the door, and from time to time he glanced that way, past my head and over the back of the booth.

All at once tears came into his eyes and his chin, patchy with unshaven fuzz, began to quiver.

"I should have gone for help that night," he said. "Just not hurting you wasn't enough."

"You're damn right," I said.

"I was scared. Honest to God, Mr. Sherris, I didn't know they were going to do what they did. I kept thinking they'd stop, but it seemed like once they got started——"

"Yes," I said. "I know."

The hamburgers came. He sat looking at them as though he had forgotten what they were.

"Go ahead and eat," I told him. "That's all over and done. You've got to think now and you can't do it well on an empty stomach."

Hunger got the better of him. He began to wolf down the food. When he was through with that I ordered more. It worked like magic. Visibly he relaxed and the gaunt twisted look in his face softened. When he reached the last hamburger I decided he was in shape to talk to.

"Do you trust me now?" I asked him. "Do you believe I'm playing fair with you?"

"I guess so," he said. "Yes."

"Well, you ought to," I told him, "because the police have been looking for you since yesterday, Adolph."

I was all ready to reach over and grab him if he tried to run. He didn't. He stiffened in his seat and the scary look came back into his eyes, but he stayed.

I explained to him exactly what the situation was and how it had come about, where he stood, and what the other boys were doing.

"You may have got out of touch these last five days," I said. "Did you know the body was found in the strip mine?"

He was white around the gills again. He seemed to shrink and double up in his seat.

"I saw it in a paper," he said. "It mentioned your name. That's when I made up my mind to call you. But you weren't there. I knew I ought to warn you what Chuck would do." He put his hands up over his face. "That's been the trouble all along, Mr. Sherris. I've known every minute what I ought to do. I was just too scared."

"Do you know what you ought to do?"

"Yes."

"Are you going to do it?"

He took his hands away from his face and looked at me. His eyes were blue. They were not particularly beautiful in size, color, or shape, but they should have been clear and zestful, a

164

boy's eyes in a boy's face. They were not, They were old and haunted. They were tired. They were heartbreaking. If I had hated him as much as the others before I could not have been able to hate him then.

"Will they hang me," he asked, "Mr. Sherris?"

I shook my head. "I won't say you're not in trouble, Bill. But it's more Chuck's worry. He did run Finelli off the road, didn't he?"

Bill shivered. "He was driving. We were all crazy, account of what had happened. Scared. You know. I saw this other car following us away from the strip mine, and Chuck saw it too. All of a sudden Chuck swerved over and slammed on the brakes, and the other car had to swing out to keep from hitting us. It went right off the curve, *fast*. Roy went down to see if the man was dead—— It was Roy killed the man in the strip mine. He's kind of nuts. He likes to hurt people. He hit the man too hard."

Bill started to get up. "I'm sick," he said. "I shouldn't have eaten all those hamburgers."

"Sit down," I told him, and he sat. "You're not going to be sick, you haven't time for that. Listen, Bill. You ran away——"

"They said they'd kill me if I ever told anybody. They said I'd hang. And there were two men dead."

"You ran away," I said, "but you didn't run very far. You had courage enough for that, Bill. You had courage enough to call me. You know what you're going to do, don't you? You've really known ever since Sunday morning but you've been stalling it off. Isn't that so?"

He thought about it, searching my face with those ancient eyes.

"I guess so," he said at last. And then, "Will you help me, Mr. Sherris? I didn't help you. I got no right to ask it, I know that. But I thought if you'd tell the police I never touched you——"

"They already know that. I'll do all I can for you, Bill, but what you do is the most important. If you go to the police voluntarily and tell them a straight story, they'll listen to you."

"If I don't," he said, apparently voicing a thought he had had many times before, "there'll be other men dead——" He sighed and went slack in his seat, all the tension run out of him. "I'm awful tired. I haven't really slept good for four months. I guess I don't care if they do hang me, so long as I'm rid of Chuck and them. Let's go."

"Good," I said. "But there's one thing you've got to do first."

I went and paid for the hamburgers and got some change. When I motioned Bill he got up like an obedient rag doll and followed me back to a telephone that was on the wall behind the row of booths.

I got long-distance and asked for the Mall's Ford number. I could hear the phone ringing for about as long as it would take to wake up an uneasy sleeper and let her get downstairs. Then Marthe Liebendorffer answered.

"This is Sherris," I said, "and I've got somebody here that wants to talk to you."

I handed the phone to Bill.

He didn't have much to say, except that he was all right and had been all right and was going to be all right, and to tell Mom he was sorry if she had worried. I could hear Marthe's voice, but not what she said. Bill said, "I know, I know, I'm sorry." I took the phone back before he started to cry. Marthe, on the other end, was already doing it.

"Listen," I said, "will you call somebody at Headquarters— I don't know who you can get at this hour, but it doesn't matter— and tell them we're on our way? Tell them your brother is coming in voluntarily. Will you do that? And then call my wife at the Ohio Hotel and tell her I'm okay."

She said she would do that, and sobbed, and then I could hear her calling to her mother that it was Adolph and he was all right. She said something more to me that I couldn't understand and hung up. I hung up, too, and turned around.

"Okay," I said. "Let's go."

Bill was standing facing the door and the single window in the front. He was staring that way, his mouth hanging open and his eyes absolutely blank with terror.

"For God's sake," I said. "What is it?"

"Somebody was looking in at us," he said. "I thought it was Bobby Stillman."

22

I LOOKED at the window and the glass door. They were empty now, showing nothing but the street and the dimly lighted store fronts on the opposite side, the occasional car, the occasional passer-by.

"Are you sure?" I said.

"I thought I was."

"But you're not sure."

"I only caught a glimpse. He was backing away. It looked like him."

The counterman smoked a cigarette, leaning on the end of the counter and talking with a seedy man who was nursing a cup of coffee. The window was blank. The door was blank. It was quiet. So quiet I could hear the blood rushing and pounding in my head.

Two boys in jeans and leather jackets strolled by outside the window, walking tough, with cigarettes in their fingers.

"There," I said. "It was one of them you saw."

"Maybe."

"Or some other boy. God damn it, how could it be Bobby Stillman? How could they have followed me?"

Bill shook his head. His shoulders moved uneasily.

"Well, let's go," I said. "Here, there's a back way."

We went out the back door into an alley. All alleys look alike. I had never realized that before. They are dark with a darkness that has nothing to do with night but is akin to that of old cellars and the places under rocks. They are dirty and drab, and people live up over them, putting cheap red curtains in the windows and red geraniums in pots on the sills to pretend that there is a little light and cheer there. Alleys all smell alike, too, of sour stinking water and old garbage. We stood on the edge of this one and looked up and down, and we didn't see anything except some lighted windows overhead and a cat going spring-footed among the puddles.

"Come on," I said. "There's nothing."

We walked along the brick pavement, beaten and broken down by trucks, patched with asphalt. The night air was cool. The canned, professional sound of a woman singing came from one of the apartments. We passed the back entrance of a tavern, in a burst of warm beery air and convivial voices. I walked as fast as I could. Bill slunk beside me, his shoulders drawn down, his head moving from side to side, craning to see behind him.

We came out on the street. People were moving up and down, not many people at this hour, but enough to keep the street from being deserted. There were a few couples, but mostly single men, an occasional drunk, a belated workman, some of the town types who don't seem to have any homes and don't care when they get back to them. I did not see any boys. It was pleasant to get back where there were lights and store windows. The Diamond was only a block away. We walked toward it, and Bill still peered over his shoulder and around.

"See anything of them?"

"No. No, I don't."

"You were mistaken."

"I guess so."

His voice carried hope but no conviction.

We walked along the Diamond to the post office, where my car was parked. I unlocked it, and we got in, and I started it. We drove off, around the Civil War monument with the iron soldier on the top. Nothing happened.

"Keep an eye out," I said. "If you see Chuck's car following us, let me know."

He hunched around, twisting so that he could see out the back window.

I headed west on 422 in thin traffic.

"There's headlights," Bill said.

"There are other cars on the road, you know."

"Yeah. It's hard to tell at night."

"That's another thing," I said. "How could Chuck and the others follow a car at night anyway? They can't have all the powers of the devil."

"Mr. Finelli followed us," said Bill.

"Sure. But that was his job. He'd had years of experience at it. And even so, he had to keep so close that you spotted him. There's nobody that close to us. There wasn't on the way over, either."

He did not dispute me. He went on looking out the back window, his chin on his hands, his hands folded on the top of the seat.

We got out beyond the drive-in theater, the markets and the eating places that fringed the town. We got out where it was dark and quiet, with nothing on either side of the road but open country, with now and again a secondary road leading off among the fields, past unlighted houses where the farmers slept against the morning milking. I stepped it up.

Headlights came swooping up the road behind me. "Watch out," said Bill, in a high whimpering voice. "Watch out." The headlights rushed at express-train speed. Abruptly they dimmed, brightened, dimmed, and brightened again. "They're going to pass," I said. A horn tooted and the car went by. It must have been doing eighty. "It isn't Chuck's car," said Bill. When it swung back in front of me my own brights picked up a fleeting glimpse of a red-and-black rear end. Then even the taillights were gone around a bend of the road.

My hands were shaking on the wheel. "God!" I said to Bill. "Will you relax? We'll be there pretty soon."

"Of course," said Bill slowly, as though he had not heard me at all, "he might not be using his own car. He might figure you'd recognize it. He might have got another one."

The road surface hummed under the tires. The wind whistled at the windows. A large sign whipped by, welcoming me to Ohio.

He might have got another one.

"Where?" I said. "The three of them are supposed to be in Cook's Forest. They couldn't borrow from their families or friends. Besides, how would Chuck know in advance that he was going to follow me?"

"He wouldn't have to know very long ahead," said Bill. "And he wouldn't have to borrow. Everett and Bobby both have hooked cars before and never got caught. And he's got Bobby with him."

"That's just great," I said. Now I was not afraid of only one specific car, a gray convertible. I was afraid of every car on the road.

I stepped it up some more. I wanted very much to be back in Mall's Ford where there were lights and people.

"So they steal cars too," I said. "What for?"

Bill shrugged. "Just to show they can."

"What do they do with them?"

"Joy-ride around, and then leave 'em somewhere. Then they brag about it afterward to the other kids."

Well, you read about that in the papers every day too. Kids picked up riding around in a stolen car. Grown men steal a car *for* something—to sell it, to make a getaway, to take them somewhere. Kids do it just to show they can.

"Is that why your friends beat up people—just to show they can?"

Bill was a long time answering that. Then he said, "It makes 'em feel big."

I suppose it would. I suppose you would feel ten feet high, standing over a man lying flat on the ground.

"How did you ever get mixed up with such a gang?" I asked him.

His voice was heavy and bitter when he spoke, not like a boy's voice at all. "I thought Chuck was God," he said. "He's big and he's smart and he's good-looking, and the girls are all crazy for him. He's good at sports. And there wasn't another guy around that dared to stand up to him."

"Did they like him?"

"Not the fellas, no. But I didn't think that mattered. I wanted to be part of his gang. I wanted the other guys to give me room when I walked in. I wanted the girls to hang around me. I——"

He paused, as though he had choked on the memory of his own folly. I got the picture clearly enough. Gawky Adolph trotting after Chuck with open mouth and eyes bugging in admiration. Chuck would love that. He'd take him on just for the laughs.

Bill said suddenly in a burst of adult and purely masculine rage, "Mom always treats me like such a goddamn baby. If my dad had lived he'd have wanted me to grow up, but Mom'd still have me in diapers if she could."

Another set of headlights came up rapidly from behind.

A semitrailer wearing festoons of yellow lights like a Christmas tree approached from the other direction, heading east. The car behind me hung back. It was a dark sedan. I could see it in the reflection from the truck's headlights. I could not, of course, see who was in it. It was the only car behind me as far as I could look back down the road.

The truck went by, and now there was nothing ahead of me, either way. The eastbound lane was clear of passing.

The car behind me still hung back.

"What's he waiting for?" I asked, getting nervous again.

A yellow highway marker popped up, with a black arc painted on it indicating a curve ahead. A straight line joined the arc, like a spear thrust into the side of a snake. A secondary road. The white center line on my left had acquired an auxiliary yellow stripe, meaning no passing.

The car behind me suddenly decided to ignore that and go around.

We were both traveling fast. Instinctively I slammed on my brakes to let the damn fool get around before something came the other way, and through the squealing of the tires I heard Bill's frantic cry, "He's cutting in on you——"

I wasn't going to be able to slow down in time.

The road swung in front of me. White guard posts, cable, a row of trees. Just like Finelli, and they'll come down to see if we're dead, and if we're not they'll make sure, and the Highway Department will place us on the list of the year's fatalities. The dark speeding flank of the other car forced me over and over, my right-hand wheels were skidding and tearing on the berm. The sedan's taillights made a baleful glaring to show me where not more than an inch of air separated our fenders, and I could swerve in and hit them and send us all over the bank but I wanted to live. Beside me, Bill was frozen in an attitude of screaming, but not a sound came out.

The subsidiary road opened up a gray gap of gravel and I went into it.

I almost did not make it. The road was narrow and built up on a low causeway. There were guards on both sides, of the steel-fender type. I shot rocking and screeching over the gravel, doing everything I could not to turn over, and I didn't turn over but I couldn't keep the car from slewing. We hit the guard with a mighty crash and rebounded, and now a new sound was added. The left rear fender was crumpled in against the wheel.

Back on the highway the sedan was fishtailing around the curve, burning rubber.

I had my car under control again. I tramped on the gas, and we barreled away down the road, but it was not going to work. The rear wheel dragged against the fender. I tried to ignore it and make the damn thing go anyway, as far as it would.

"Do you see any place?" I asked Bill. "A house?"

The road lifted up a grade. Bill bent forward. I could feel him shaking.

"There's something up there at the top," he said. "I think. A barn."

"Well, if there's a barn, there'll be a house near it. We can get help." I pushed the accelerator as hard and as far as I could, and the car staggered about halfway up the hill, and the tire blew.

"They've turned around," said Bill, looking back.

"All right," I said. "God damn them, let them."

I left the car where it died, in the middle of the road, blocking it. I turned the lights off. I hoped they would ram into it at full speed. "We'd better get away from here," I said.

We went over the ditch and into the field. I couldn't see any sign of a house, but the barn stood plainly on top of the rise, a big dark bulk against the sky. Too big even for a barn, I thought, but it was the shape of one, and I couldn't think what else it would be.

In the distance there was the sound of a car making a turn at high speed onto gravel. There were trees between us now, but I could see the headlights through them, moving fast.

"What are we going to do?" asked Bill, and his voice was so tight and small that I could hardly hear it.

But it was a good question.

The field was wide and open and the barn looked miles away, and I was in no shape for cross-country running.

"Listen," I said, "the house must be on the other side. You run like hell and find it." I wanted him safe, out of the way. "I've got a gun."

"Chuck's got one too," said Bill. "A little old target rifle. If he's got it with him."

And he probably would have.

"Well," I said, "go on anyway. We need someone to call the cops."

"No," he said. "We'll go together."

He grabbed my elbow and we humped it, through the sweet-smelling late-summer grass. I could hear the wheels of the sedan churning up the hill. It did not hit my car. They stopped in time. After that the countryside was quiet, very serene, very peaceful, with nothing to disturb it but the monotonous love song of the crickets.

We made it to the barn.

There was a wide graveled space in front of it like a parking area, and there were several signs around, but it did not have any of the normal appurtenances of a farmyard. I looked up at the high blank wall, painted white, glimmering faintly under the stars. There were letters on it, big and black. Even in this darkness I could make out the size and shape of words, enough to guess the sense of them.

This was a sale barn, a place where livestock was sold at auction once or twice a week. At other times it was empty. And there would not necessarily be a house anywhere near it.

There was no house.

I leaned up against the plank wall, but not for long. Bill caught my shoulder and pointed. The road was only forty or fifty feet away. Someone in a light shirt was running on it. I looked around and made out two more moving shapes, one in the field the way we had just come, and one on the other side of the road. I took the gun out of my pocket and clicked the safety back. There was now no chance of Bill getting away unseen. He was safer to stay with me.

"Find a door," I said, "Break it open. Or a window. Get inside and then let me in. This is a sale barn, they ought to have a phone." I could make out wires overhead, but it was impossible to distinguish between phone and power lines. "Get with it," I said.

Bill scuttled around the corner of the building. I followed after him, more slowly. I watched the three moving shapes in the starlit night. Here we are again, I thought, and something evil and savage woke up in me. This time I wasn't helpless. This time I was armed.

The young tigers padded closer in the night.

One of them, the light-shirted one in the road, called out to me, "Sherris!"

It was Chuck's voice. It had a dark thick note of pleasure in it. I was standing just at the corner of the barn now. Behind me I could hear Bill slamming around in hurried desperation. There was a smashing noise. I said to Chuck, "Look out, yellowbelly. I've got a gun."

"Well, now," said Chuck. "And so have I."

But it wasn't Chuck at all that had the gun. It was the boy coming up through the field, at my right side.

He missed me. I heard the bullet go by, singing, and almost in the same second I fired at the place where the crack and flash had come from. The night had turned black, there were no stars in it, no road, no countryside, no white wall behind me. There were three shadows in it, in three different places, and these I could see, but nothing else. I fired at them.

And they were gone.

23

B<small>ILL</small> was pulling at me. "Come on," he said. "Come on, I've got the door open."

I pushed him off. I had almost forgotten who he was.

"No," I said. "They're dead. I've killed them."

The night was black. There was wind in it. It shook me. It was loud. I shouted to make myself heard above it.

"I killed them!" I shouted, and I was glad. I wanted to see the bodies. I wanted to maul them. I remembered Tracey with the blood on her face, and I wanted to kick and tear and destroy them, to stamp them into the earth. I started to walk away from the barn.

Bill cried, "Please! Please." His voice was shrill. "Hell," he said, "are you crazy? They aren't dead."

He dragged me by main force around the corner.

I caught the wall. "They aren't?" I said.

"Hell, no. They just ducked. They were on the ground before you even fired. Come *on*."

He hustled me through a door. Now it was pitch dark, but normally so. The smell of blood and gunsmoke was replaced by a heavy ingrained odor of sweet hay and cow manure. I stood trembling, but not in any wind of passion. I was just tired and cold, with all that heat run out of me.

I thought, For a minute I was no better than they are. For a minute there——

And I was still no better. I still had the vision of their bodies lying on the ground, and I was sorry it wasn't so. I was sorry that I hadn't killed them.

I felt sick. I almost dropped the gun.

Bill was thumping futilely with the door. "I can't lock it," he panted. "I broke it with a big stone and it won't stay shut."

I leaned my back against it. "See if you can find a light switch."

"What about windows?" he protested. "They can see in."

"I don't think there are any on the ground floor," I said, squinting to see paler squares against the black. "They're all higher up. Go on, we can't bumble around in the dark."

"All right," he said, unconvinced. I could hear him feeling up and down the wall. In a minute there was a click, and we were blinded with light.

We blinked at each other like owls, and we felt exposed, but it was good even so. I was fed up with dark and shadows and the unhealthy things that hide in them. There were wooden benches around the wall. We dragged some of them up to help block the door. Then we looked around.

I had been right about the windows. They were all too high to be dangerous. A narrow balcony with folding chairs in it hung on three sides of the barn, reached by a steep flight of wooden stairs. On the ground floor were the benches, and plenty of room for men to stand and look over the railing into the semicircular pit where the stock was brought in. There was a stand there for the auctioneer, and at the back of the pit were big double doors leading into the stable shed. The rough board walls were covered with fly-specked posters advertising feeds and milkers and remedies for mastitis.

There were two doors in the inner wall. One was at the back, with the word MEN painted on it. The other one was on the opposite side of the pit. It was marked OFFICE.

"That's where the phone would be," I said, "if there is one."

We started for it, but we didn't make it. We weren't even close. There must have been a ground-floor window in the office, because we heard it break. We heard a great hustling of bodies climbing in and then more noises in the office.

There had been a phone in the office. There was not now. The boys had taken care of it.

Bill had got small again. He had a peculiar way of shrinking in, drawing his lanky frame together. His face had no color in it. I pointed to the stairs and he went up them in about three wild bounds. I didn't go so fast.

It had grown quiet in the office now.

The door opened, not very far, enough for a cautious eye to see through.

I was halfway up the stairs, a sitting bird if they used the rifle. Even a light-caliber bullet is nothing to fool with, especially at close range. I put a shot in the wall beside the office door and it slammed shut again.

I clambered the rest of the way up to the balcony and lay down on it. I had an open front, with a fence-type railing. I had the strategic position now. I had five bullets left.

I wondered how I was going to use them.

Bill lay beside me between the overturned folding chairs on the bare floor, with the splinters and the dust and the dried rinds of mud and barnyard dirt fallen off the boots of farmers. After a while he whispered, "It's awful quiet. Where are they?"

I shook my head.

"Do you think they've gone?"

"I doubt it," I said, and wished to God they had.

I was getting a violent reaction. Now I was glad I hadn't killed them, or even hurt them, and I didn't want to be tempted again.

This was foolish, perhaps. If I killed all three of them it would be in self-defense and in defense of Bill. We were on the right side. Nobody would blame us.

But I didn't want to do it. I didn't want to be put in a position where I could do it.

You know why?

Because I lusted to kill them. Now, in the full light, in the coolness of reaction, I lusted to kill them. I never wanted anything so much since the day I was born. I wanted it beyond justice or reason or self-preservation.

The tiger stripes were showing on my own hide.

The office door burst open. Swiftly, suddenly, in one leap, Chuck was out and under the edge of the balcony, back in the one place where I couldn't cover him. He had the rifle now, in his own hand.

Roy Aspinwall came beside him, his indispensable shadow. I would have had to kill Roy to get at Chuck. I imagine Chuck had planned it that way.

Bobby Stillman came third. And he lost his nerve.

He started to leap from the dark office into the light, and it was as though the light was a barrier, driving him back. I saw him look up at the balcony, at me. I knew what he was thinking. He was thinking of the bullet hole beside the door, close beside where his head was now. Maybe he was remembering another bullet that had come looking for him in the dark outside, and thinking that a third one would not miss. Maybe he was thinking that it was an ill thing altogether to be shot at.

He froze halfway through the office door, his back against the jamb, his hands flung out and feeling along the wall for something, I don't know what. Salvation, perhaps.

Chuck screamed, "Come on, God damn you, jump!"

"Sure," I said, "come on, Bobby. What's the matter, don't you like the light? Don't you like it when you can't sneak up from behind?"

He didn't like it. I could see his face, the undistinguished, nondescript face of the photograph, but now with terror added, with a cringing whiteness, with glassy eyes looking from me to Chuck, from Chuck to me again.

He was a perfect target. I couldn't miss. I could drop him on the floor with one shot and watch him kick.

The sweat ran in my eyes, and I wiped it with my left hand. "Get out," I told him. "Get the hell out while you live."

He broke and ran. For a second or two I could hear him floundering in the office, his shoes scrunching on the broken window glass. Chuck yelled after him, "Chicken! Chicken!" But he was out the window and gone.

"All right," I said, "yellowbelly. Let's see how brave you are."

Chuck told me obscenely to shut up.

There was silence again in the barn.

Bill moved his head close to my ear. "They're whispering down there. I can hear them——"

"Keep down," I said. "Move back from the edge and keep down." I pushed him away. "Chuck," I said. "Chuck Landry. You're behind the times. We've known who you were since Wednesday. The cops are already on your tail."

He was talking hard and fast to Roy. He pretended he didn't hear me. He pretended he didn't care. Maybe he didn't.

"You're a real smart boy," I said. "Two killings on your hands already, and you want to make it two more. How do you think you're going to cover that one now?"

Now he answered me, contemptuous, sure of himself. Proud.

"Easy," he said. "Put your bodies in your car and shove it in the ditch and burn it. It'll still look like an accident."

"With our bodies full of .22 slugs?"

"I'll leave the rifle in Bill's hands and say he stole it from me. It'll give the police something to occupy their dim brains."

There was hardly any sound to warn me. Roy had taken his shoes off. He had crept to the other end of the balcony and now he whipped around the end post and was on the stairs. I couldn't see him or shoot at him without raising up, and the minute I raised up or moved Chuck would step out and let me have it with the rifle.

"What's he got with him?" I asked. "A pocket full of stones and a slingshot?"

No answer.

I could hear Roy on the stairs, creeping up one step at a time on all fours, panting and snuffling with eager excitement.

"There's only one hitch in your plan, Chuck," I said. "How are you going to explain Roy's body? Because I'm going to kill him the minute he shows his thick head over that top step."

The movement on the stairs stopped. Roy was not very bright, but even a moron can understand a simple statement like that. I motioned to Bill and he slid up on his belly to where I could whisper in his ear.

Chuck said, "Go ahead, Roy. He can't hurt you."

"Yes, come ahead, Roy," I said. "You'll find out."

I spoke to Bill and he nodded and began to squirm away toward the top of the steps, keeping down flat.

Roy said, doubtfully, "Hey, Chuck——"

I moved closer to the edge of the balcony.

"Go on," said Chuck furiously, "what are you scared of? I've got you covered."

"He's scared of dying," I said. "Aren't you, Roy? And you should be. Sure, he's got you covered. The minute I raise up to shoot you, he'll shoot me. But that won't save your life, will it?"

Bill was almost within reach of the stair now.

"Anyway," I said to Chuck, "what are *you* scared of, yellow-belly? I don't see you risking your tender skin."

Bill was making more noise now, and I raised my voice. It did not take any effort of acting.

"What's the matter with you both?" I shouted. "I don't hear you laughing and cracking funny jokes, like you did before. This isn't so much fun, is it, when I'm ready and waiting for you?"

Bill shied a folding chair down the stairs with a crash and a rattle. He threw another and another, and Roy yelped, and when the fourth one hit him he scuttered back down the stairs. I put a bullet in the floor beside him as he came around the post. I meant to miss him.

I think.

Chuck did not mean to miss me but he did, firing from an angle under the balcony where he could not possibly have hit me.

The two shots made a tremendous noise in the place, and then there was another interval of absolute stillness while we all crouched and breathed and waited.

Into the stillness, faintly, from far off, a little sound came trickling.

The sound of sirens.

We listened to it.

It grew, coming closer.

"Hey," said Roy. "That's cops."

The sound turned, audibly and unmistakably, from the distant highway into the secondary road.

Chuck fired at the lights in the center of the ceiling. There was a cluster of them set in round white reflectors. He broke three of them before he ran out his magazine. Two of them still burned.

He dropped the rifle and made a run for the office door.

I put a bullet in the wall ahead of him.

He dropped into a crouch and whirled and darted back under the balcony. The sirens came wailing along the road.

Roy said, "Hey, Chuck, what'll we do? I thought you said——"

But Chuck was running.

I heard his feet pound over the wooden floor, and then he tried it again, this time from the other end of the balcony, toward the door Bill and I had come through. He started to tear and heave at the benches that blocked it.

I put a shot in the panel of the door.

He turned again. He was a big tall handsome boy, but he was not standing tall now, and the beauty of his face was something less than skin deep. He was afraid, and with him fear was a disease that twisted him out of all normal semblance.

He sprang over the railing into the pit and ran across the trodden dirt and straw to the double doors.

I put a shot over his shoulder, and he winced from the flying splinters and the nearness of death.

He stopped where he was, and I said, "I've got one left, Chuck."

"You won't shoot me," he said. "You didn't shoot Bobby. You let him go."

"Try it," I said.

He stood with his hands outstretched, hooked onto the edge of one door. It was loose and ready to swing. Beyond it was the darkness of the stable shed, and possible escape. All Chuck needed was one fast step, and the guts to take it.

I lay watching the broad of his back. There were tears in my eyes, I wanted to shoot him so bad. So bad.

He did not take the step.

He let go of the door rather slowly. His head came around, as though drawn by the fascination of the cold round eye of my gun. Then his whole body turned, and then he began to shake. He bent down onto one knee and put a hand on the ground to steady himself and he stayed there. His eyes had become perfectly blank in a face as stiff and unreal as a painted mask.

Roy came padding on his sock feet out from under the balcony, carrying his shoes. He seemed to have forgotten all about me. He went hesitantly to the railing of the pit and looked over it.

"Chuck," he said. "Hey, Chuck . . .?"

The police came in.

24

THE way in which the boys had known I was at my house was childishly simple. Literally. They had subsidized the boy up the street, the one with the bicycle and the brown-and-white dog. They had got the boy alone, and Roy had hurt his dog a little to show what would happen to the dog if he didn't do as he was told. Then they gave him some nickels and a phone number. They set him to watch my house and call them the minute I came back.

He had called them, of course, and they had come and set up watch themselves, still using the boy as liaison. When I stayed on and on, and it got dark, and I still stayed with the lights out, it became obvious that I was waiting for something, and Chuck guessed what the something was—either Bill in person, or a call from him. Bill had unwisely threatened once before to come to me, and that was when they had given him the bruises his sister had mentioned.

If Bill came himself, they could grab him. But if I went to meet him, they wanted to be able to follow. So Bobby sneaked into my garage and cracked the red lens of one of the tail-lights on my car, so it would show a white streak, making it easy for them.

They had had another boy similarly staked out on Bill's home. If he had come there, they would have got him. Meanwhile, they were holding out in a roadside camp by a small fishing lake five miles from Mall's Ford, staying out of sight by day and roaming by night.

It almost worked.

The phone call Bill and I made from Newbridge had brought the police looking for us. Koleski, working all hours on his holdup, had been at Headquarters, when Marthe Liebendorffer and he decided to take time off to be sure we made it. When he and Hartigan didn't meet us on the road, and it was fairly sure that something had held us up, he radioed the nearest highway-patrol car and started to scour the country. The sales barn stood on a high rise, and the lights from its windows showed a long way.

So that was that. My tigers were caged, and the shadow of terror that Tracey and I had lived under for more than four months was lifted. We moved back to our own house, and the kids played in their own yard, and we stopped, eventually, shivering every time a fast car went by or the wind shook the trees at night.

So what does it all prove?

You tell me.

The legal business went on longer, much longer, than the chase. With Roy Aspinwall it was simple. The psychiatrists took one look at him and sent him away to a suitable institution. His parents admitted that they had had trouble with him before. They had had to move several times because of Roy's activities, with smaller children and animals. But they kept hoping—— They were decent people. All they wanted to do was protect their son. Who can blame them? Certainly not Finelli. Not Artie Clymer.

Everett Bush was lucky. All he had against him was aggravated assault, and I was the only one to prosecute. He cried and said Chuck led him into it and he was afraid to stop, like Bill. They gave him a year in the Boys' Industrial School, sentence suspended pending good behavior. I don't know whether he's behaved or not. I haven't seen him since. I hope he has. I hope he's learned his lesson. And I hope his parents take more interest now in what he does and who he runs with, instead of merely lying to protect him after it's too late, as they did before. But I doubt it. They seemed more angry with me for bringing the whole thing up and making trouble about it than they were with Everett for doing it.

Bobby Stillman was picked up just down the road from the barn that night and pretty soon he was trying to give evidence faster and louder than Bill, to get himself off the hook. He was a slimy kid. He came from a fairly wealthy family and he seemed to have been alternately spoiled and neglected by a silly mother and a father who figured that a big allowance was the answer to all child care, but this didn't seem to account for his turning vicious. At least not to me. Anyway, he talked fast, and his father talked faster, and it turned out that none of it was really Bobby's fault, he was forced into it and just went along for the ride. One year, suspended.

Bill got off light, too, and that was fair enough. We're good friends. He does yard work for us, and he runs to me with his problems as though I was his father. I know he's stayed out of trouble. He'd never have got into it in the first place if he hadn't been so young and simple that a phony like Chuck could take him in.

But Chuck found himself on a harder road. He was eighteen and stood trial as an adult. And he couldn't talk himself out of it quite so easily. Roy had actually killed Clymer, but Chuck was the avowed leader of the gang. Chuck had engineered that accident that killed Finelli. Chuck had attempted to kill me with slugs fired from a hunting-type slingshot. Chuck had done a lot of things and he didn't have anybody to hide behind.

Except his parents.

They had money. They spent it for him. He had the best lawyers there were. They fought like lions to keep him out of prison. They had two other kids, a boy and a girl, both apparently nice normal youngsters, but Chuck was the crooked one and somehow more precious for that reason, or more vulnerable and so more in need of protection. They were decent people. This was their son. They wanted to help him. Again, who could blame them?

I could. I could blame them for shutting their eyes, like the Aspinwalls, to something they knew but would not face.

They admitted that Chuck had always been "different," moody and withdrawn, preferring to play secret games by himself or to sit in a dark corner and daydream. He did not get along well with other children when he was small. He was too intelligent for his age group. He was also too bossy. He had to order and domineer, and if anyone refused to obey him he would fly into furious tantrums. He could not endure to have his will crossed or his actions criticized. But he was such a handsome boy, so able in his studies, so bright, so full of promise——

He was a sadist too. Not in the crude physical way that Roy was, but subtly tormenting, choosing out smaller and weaker children and making life hell for them in ways they did not know how to combat. His own brother and sister testified to that. It was obvious that they feared and hated him. They also admitted that Chuck had always hated his parents because they were bigger than he when he was a child, and later because they still exerted some authority over him. Nobody, but nobody could be bigger than Chuck Landry, or tell him what to do.

He and his parents seemed eventually to have reached a sort of tacit compromise, wherein he pretended to be a good and dutiful son, and they pretended to believe it. This avoided the scenes, the rages, the bitter sulking. They could stop worrying and he could let his hatred slide off into contempt—contempt for everything they stood for, for suburbia, for the solid undistinguished manner in which most people spend their lives, for husbands who cut the lawn when their wives asked them to. None of this was for Chuck. He was big. He was—different.

He was also a physical coward, and the psychiatrists had a lot of theories about how this was probably one of his basic troubles. He saw himself as perfect, had to see himself that way, but every time some resentful playmate threatened to poke him one he knew he was not perfect, because he could not fight on anything like even terms. So he had to bolster himself up with a gang of lackwits and go around acting like a king, compensating for the flaw.

Then, through the chain of circumstances that began that night at Noddy's, Chuck discovered his true forte. Safe in size and numbers, he could play something bigger than a king. When he beat me up, as means of re-establishing his importance after the ignominious failure of the foray into Beekman Street, he felt more big, more beautiful, more powerful and perfect than

186

he ever had before. This was greater than tormenting children. This was the real true stuff, and hovering beyond it, veiled as yet but seductive, was the promise of the greatest act af all, the actual taking of human life.

Power. Violence gave it to him, and he loved it. He loved it the way another kid loves girls, or building hot rods, or playing ball. Through violence Chuck was able for the first time in his sterile life to create.

Crazy?

The defense said so. The prosecution said not. The prosecution said Chuck had a psychopathic personality, but was not psychotic. He knew perfectly well the difference between right and wrong. He simply didn't care.

And all through the trial Chuck remained as cool and unmoved as a chunk of marble. The most they could do on Finelli was second-degree, and so he had no death penalty to be afraid of. He would not admit anything. He scoffed politely at all the testimony, accusing us all of lying. He seemed perfectly secure in the belief that he was going to get away with it because he was Chuck Landry and for him there was no other possibility.

In a sense he did get away with it. He had very good lawyers. He was sentenced to from five to twenty years, which means he'll be out again in five even if his appeal fails. This is supposed to teach him the error of his ways. I hope it will. But I wonder. Watching his face, trying to penetrate to the strange cold recesses behind it, I wonder if anything ever will. I have a curious feeling of defeat.

So that's that. My personal troubles in this connection are over. My wife and I have a finer relationship based on what we went through together. My leg is pretty well healed up now, and I only limp a bit in wet weather. The doctor says even this will clear up in time, or almost. And after all, what are four or five months out of a lifetime?

Artie Clymer is dead, but he didn't amount to much, anyway. Some other tramps got beaten up. And Finelli, a good man, is dead, but men die every day, and the water closes over their heads, and the world goes on. And what are you going to do about it?

Apparently nothing.

But, damn it, something ought to be done.

I don't have the answer. I do have two kids, and it's up to me to see that they grow up to be decent members of society. Maybe if I realized that Pudge had an evil kink in him that no ordinary training could eradicate, I would be reluctant, too, to face it. But I think I would have to, remembering that night when I lay in the weeds on Williams Avenue.

I think sooner or later we'll have to find the answer. Because we all live closer together now, more interdependent and intertwined than ever before, and the tiger is flourishing among us.

Every day you read of his casual violence and its victims. But, of course, you don't think you'll be the next one.

I didn't think so, either.

b l u e   m u r d e r

☐	LEIGH BRACKETT	No Good From A Corpse	£3.95
☐		The Tiger Among Us	£3.95
☐	GIL BREWER	13 French Street & The Red Scarf	£4.50
☐	DAVID GOODIS	The Burglar	£3.50
☐	DAVIS GRUBB	The Night of the Hunter	£3.50
☐	DOLORES HITCHENS	Sleep With Slander	£3.95
☐		Sleep With Strangers	£3.95
☐	GEOFFREY HOMES	Build My Gallows High	£3.95
☐	WILLIAM P. MCGIVERN	The Big Heat	£3.50
☐	JOEL TOWNSLEY ROGERS	The Red Right Hand	£3.95
☐	NEWTON THORNBURG	Cutter and Bone	£3.95
☐	CHARLES WILLIAMS	The Diamond Bikini	£3.50
☐	CORNELL WOOLRICH	Rear Window and Other Stories	£4.50

All these books are available at your local bookshop or newsagent, or can be ordered direct from the publisher. Just tick the titles you want and fill in the form below.

Prices and availability subject to change without notice.

Blue Murder Paperbacks, P.O. Box 11, Falmouth, Cornwall.

Please send cheque or postal order, and allow the following for postage and packing:

U.K. – 60p for one book, plus 25p for the second book, and 15p for each additional book ordered up to a maximum of £1.90.

Overseas (including EIRE) – £1.25 for the first book, plus 75p for the second, and 28p for each additional book thereafter.

Name ....

Address ....

....

....

....

....